PAGES BOOK EMPORIUM
1011 BAKER ST.
CRANBROOK, B.C. V1C 1A6
PH: 489-3262

Cinnamon Knew She Was Crazy To Play Games.

"I told you once before, I'm no gentleman," Ben said.

"And I told you, you couldn't have fooled me," Cinnamon replied tartly.

"What makes you think I can't keep you off balance? I can still sneak up on you."

"You're warning me again. Why? I don't need warnings." But some instinct for survival was alerted in her.

"The hunt is always more stimulating when the quarry knows that there are traps."

"You're likely to lose this game with a philosophy like that," Cinnamon countered.

Ben inclined his head, acknowledging her words. "Maybe. But before I worry about that I'm going to kiss you. Are you going to bite or do something equally unpleasant?"

"Try and see."

D0206431

Dear Reader:

I hope you've been enjoying 1989, our "Year of the Man" at Silhouette Desire. Every one of the twelve authors who are contributing a *Man of the Month* has created a very special someone for your reading pleasure. Each man is unique, and each author's style and characterization give you a different insight into her man's story.

From January to December, 1989 will be a twelve-month extravaganza spotlighting one book each month with special cover treatment as a tribute to the Silhouette Desire hero—our *Man of the Month*!

Created by your favorite authors, these men are utterly captivating—and I think Mr. June, Annette Broadrick's Quinn McNamara, will be simply... *Irresistible*! One of Lass Small's Lambert sisters gets a very special man in July. *Man of the Month* Graham Rawlins may start as the *Odd Man Out*, but that doesn't last long....

Yours,

Isabel Swift

Senior Editor & Editorial Coordinator

SARA CHANCE
Eye of the Storm

Silhouette Desire

Published by Silhouette Books New York
America's Publisher of Contemporary Romance

SILHOUETTE BOOKS
300 East 42nd St., New York, N.Y. 10017

Copyright © 1989 by Sydney Ann Clary

All rights reserved. Except for use in any review,
the reproduction or utilization of this work in
whole or in part in any form by any electronic,
mechanical or other means, now known or
hereafter invented, including xerography,
photocopying and recording, or in any information
storage or retrieval system, is forbidden without
the permission of Silhouette Books, 300 E. 42nd St.,
New York, N.Y. 10017

ISBN: 0-373-05500-5

First Silhouette Books printing June 1989

All the characters in this book are fictitious. Any
resemblance to actual persons, living or dead, is
purely coincidental.

®: Trademark used under license and
registered in the United States Patent and
Trademark Office and in other countries.

Printed in the U.S.A.

Books by Sara Chance

Silhouette Desire

Her Golden Eyes #46
Home at Last #83
This Wildfire Magic #107
A Touch of Passion #183
Look Beyond Tomorrow #244
Where the Wandering Ends #357
Double Solitaire #388
Shadow Watch #406
To Tame the Wind #430
Southern Comfort #467
Woman in the Shadows #485
Eye of the Storm #500

SARA CHANCE

lives on Florida's Gold Coast. With the ocean two minutes from home, a boat in the water in the backyard and an indoor swimming pool three feet from her word processor, is it any wonder she loves swimming, fishing and boating? Asked why she writes romances, she replies, "I live it and believe in it. After all, I met and married my husband, David, in less than six weeks." That was two teenage daughters and twenty years ago. Two of Sara's Desires, *Her Golden Eyes* and *A Touch of Passion*, were nominated by Romantic Times in the Best Desires category for their respective publishing years. And *Double Solitaire* was a Romance Writers of America Golden Medallion nominee.

One

You're out of your damn mind. I am not taking another assignment."

Benjamin Forsythe didn't raise his voice; he didn't have to. His reputation was such that most people who knew of him, however few those were, gave him a wide berth when he spoke in that sleepy drawl. Although technically his boss, Jonathon, the man watching him, was no exception. Benjamin—"Ben" to his friends, "Apollo" to his cohorts on both sides of the international political blanket—would have laughed if he had been in the mood. Making bureaucratic twits nervous was one of the rare pleasures he allowed himself in life.

"Be reasonable."

Jonathon stifled his irritation and tried for patience. Every man in his department had a personality that seemed to go with the job he did. Apollo was one exception. The man had the most irreverent attitude. He seemed to delight in flaunting the rules and never did the expected. Jonathon would have liked an operative he could control. But he was no fool; much as Jonathon hated to admit it, Ben was the best in his field.

"I am always reasonable," Ben pointed out with marked boredom.

Jonathon flushed, then glared, his appreciation of Apollo's talent and skill disappearing at the laconic reply. Two more lousy weeks and Apollo would be out of his hair. "I can order you."

"You can try. We both know you won't." Ben shrugged, his lanky body looking curiously disjointed as he made the gesture. At first glance, nothing about his appearance inspired a second look. His body was all limbs; his face had too many angles and character lines for handsomeness. His eyes appeared as sleepy as his voice usually sounded. The visual picture he presented to the unwary observer was that of a pleasant male in his late thirties, with dusty brown hair and hazel eyes. Ben knew what he looked like— even traded on it blatantly. His remarkable skill at blending in anywhere, his photographic memory, and a mind that excelled at solving the most complex puzzles were simply tools of his trade. Added to the whole was the tenacity of a pit bulldog. The combination had lifted him to the top of his profession.

"Our superiors are very worried about this one. They have requested that you be called in. It was their decision, not mine. I'm not going to pretend at this late date that I don't find you aggravating and difficult to handle. But you get the job done. Had the choice been mine, I would have let Briggs and Jeffries keep this assignment. The bottom line is that this is the last one for you."

"Bull. You said that three months ago, and I almost ended up on a slab in a godforsaken morgue and you wouldn't have even had the decency to claim my remains." Ben had heard this argument too many times in the past to be taken in. There was always one more assignment, the vacation that never came, the R and R that inevitably got shunted aside to save the world—only the world didn't seem to want saving. It was on a self-destruct course and he wanted off.

Ben stared the older man straight in the eye. God, he was tired of the lies, the broken promises. Where had truth, justice and the American way gone? When had fighting the bad guys and protecting freedom become life in a gray fog where right and wrong wore the same face? The movies and television made heroes out of men like him and fairy tales out of hard-core reality. He was no James Bond. Columbo, maybe. He smiled a little at the thought.

Jonathon distrusted the smile. "You knew the risks."

Ben's humor died at the dry words. "I thought I did, but I'm not so sure anymore." He shifted in his chair, wondering if it was worth it to walk out on this little tête-à-tête. The damnable part was that Jonathon could order him to go on this assignment, whatever it was. And he'd go. He had two more weeks left before he was out of the business. Until then, although he was officially clearing his desk, he couldn't legitimately refuse an order.

Jonathon lifted the folder and slid it across the desk. "Just look at these. Read the dossier. That's all I'm asking. If you can't see the importance of what's in there, then you can walk—then I'll tell them you won't take the job."

Ben studied him, testing the surprising words for their veracity. He didn't like Jonathon. The man had never been in the field and had precious little savvy about its dangers or the toll the work took on its operatives. He was a pen pusher and a rear kisser as far as Ben was concerned. Then again, there really hadn't been time to find the right kind of head for the department after the fiasco involving the last director eighteen months ago. The breach in security had made Washington nervous. The powers that be had sent Jonathon in until a replacement could be found, and somehow, temporary had become permanent.

"Just one look."

"Why?" Ben was intrigued despite himself at the way Jonathon was pushing.

Jonathon sighed, wearily rubbing his neck. "I sent two other men, Briggs and Jeffries, on this case. You should know how good they are—you trained them. Neither cracked this little nut." He didn't like admitting his failure, but he had no choice.

Ben felt a ripple of something akin to interest stir— his one besetting sin, curiosity. Someone he cared for had once told him it would get him into trouble one day. He reached for the folder without taking his eyes from Jonathon's face. The director's relief was blatantly obvious.

Photographs slipped out: eight-by-ten color pictures. A woman, long-legged, narrow hipped, with deliciously curved breasts and the most glorious russet hair looked out of every shot. Smiling, intense, serious, alone, pensive. Emotions radiated from her face as sunshine spills across the land at dawn. Ben felt the shock wave of desire go straight to his midsection. Training and a natural ability to safely hide his own reactions kept his expression bland.

"Beautiful, isn't she?"

Ben heard the grudging compliment. "No." Exquisite. Unique. Exotic. And with those slanted green eyes, so sensual a man could burn up just letting his imagination have free rein. Needing to know more about the woman, Ben picked up the computer printout that should have been covered with facts. The meager single sheet stopped him cold in his mental tracks.

Birthplace: Chicago. Birthday: January twelfth. Single. Bachelor of political science from the University of Tennessee. Age: thirty. Currently aide to Senator Donald Metcalf, the newest candidate for the presidency. Valid driver's license but no personal car. No arrests, no anything.

"An unusual name...Cinnamon Cartier." Ben glanced back at the photos. "But other than that I don't see any problem. Funny, she doesn't look thirty."

"We think it's an alias, but we can't prove it."

Ben pulled his gaze from the pictures long enough to glance at Jonathon. "Why does it matter, and how deep did you dig?"

"Too deep." Jonathon rose and paced to the window. He stopped, his hands clasped behind his back. "Her history checks out in all the obvious ways. An orphan. High-school graduate, just barely. Small-time jobs, mostly under-the-table stuff. The thing is no one seems to remember her very well and nothing seems to add up to the woman she is now. Either she's a ringer or she's got some powerful backing. No one would have taken on a national campaign for a senator who had little or no public image outside his own state. Why? Why would a woman with almost no visible intelligence in high school not only enroll in college, pay in cash, and then manage to graduate in the top three of her class." He swung around, angry and frustrated. "Not three percent. Three of her class. By all accounts she's brilliant. Metcalf took her into his camp right out of college. The man's no fool despite his unknown status. Now she's his aide, handles him and his family like a seasoned political general. He leaves the details to her to concentrate on the campaign trail. It's a good partnership—some say too good.

"The thing is, when Metcalf was a relative unknown in the presidential sweepstakes, no one did more than a cursory check. Now that the guy is moving up in the ranks, people are becoming uneasy. Who is this senator out of the South who is making the big boys nervous? We haven't had the first primary yet and he's caught the eye of the nation. Every day his popularity grows. And this Cinnamon Cartier is right beside him all the way."

"Smart woman." Ben was beginning to see the concern, although he didn't view it quite so strongly. "So what if she has someone's backing?"

Jonathon glared at him. "I can do without your jokes. Or are you being deliberately obtuse? The man is smart. And she isn't your garden-variety political aide."

"I agree. The woman is definitely unique." He looked back at the photos. The senator and his family were in three of the shots. He hadn't paid much attention to them at first but this time he did. The four could have been an ad for the golden image of the all-American family. "Domestic politics isn't really my bag," he murmured finally, tossing the pictures aside. Cinnamon Cartier's face was etched too clearly in his mind for peace. He didn't like the feeling but he didn't fight it. He had learned the value of expending his energy only on necessities. If he was going to see her again, he would have controlled himself.

Jonathon glared at him and continued abruptly. "Then make it your bag. We need help on this one. The man doesn't put a foot wrong. She makes sure that the media loves him. His wife is a sweet little homebody who hasn't sent one feminist up in arms. Even his kids are models and both of them are just entering their teens, a tough age according to our psychologists. How is she doing it? More importantly, who is she doing it for? It's inconceivable that she is pulling this off on her own."

Ben was inclined to agree but he didn't say so. Instead his gaze was drawn back to the photographs. Something about them wasn't right. The emotions were too free, he realized. Camouflage. Brilliant, eye-catching camouflage. Her eyes. People could change their body language, their facial expression, even the tone of their voice; but few had complete control over their eyes.

Cinnamon had slipped. No matter what the look on her face, her eyes projected only one mood—of cool, calculating awareness. He had seen hunted wild animals with just such intense stares.

Instinct, rather than intent, governed his next words. He didn't understand the paradox of this woman, and he certainly wasn't as worried about her affiliation, best he could see the ramifications if what

Jonathon believed turned out to be true. He was puzzled and intrigued. "What do you want me to do?"

Jonathon returned to his chair, concealing his relief. "I've arranged for you to be assigned to Metcalf's security team. Think of it as a taste of the business you'll be starting when you leave us." He ignored Ben's glare to continue. "Take her apart, fill in the gaps, get the questions answered. If necessary, discredit her or whatever it takes to nullify her threat."

Ben looked up. "Putting me on security for Metcalf isn't necessarily going to mean I can dog her footsteps," he pointed out.

Jonathon met his gaze squarely. "I've never heard of Apollo failing. You'll find a way."

"And if she isn't a threat? What then? Do we apologize to the lady and tell her it was all for the sake of her country?"

Jonathon grimaced before sliding a video cassette across the desk. "Watch this tonight when you get home and you'll see just how much a threat Cinnamon Cartier is. If there is any apologizing to be done, it won't come from us. No one springs from her background and pulls off the political coup of the decade without help—help that is determined to stay hidden. The woman is covering something, and it's got to be buried deep or we would find it." He reached into his desk and withdrew a white envelope. "You'll need this, as well. It will get you in the door at the fund-raising dinner for Metcalf two days from now. In the meantime, do whatever you feel necessary while I get you transferred to security."

Ben collected the file, the tape and the invitation and got to his feet. "This is going to cost you a secretary to finish up my paperwork and clear out my desk. And I think I'd like a vacation at the company's expense, as well." Jonathon may have gotten what he wanted, but Ben had no intention of allowing him to escape scot-free.

Jonathon nodded. "Anything. Just get that woman before she can do any real damage. The last thing we need in the White House is a puppet president."

Ben could have pointed out that there were very few people in government work who weren't having their strings pulled by someone. Political favors were an accepted way of life. As far as he was concerned, politics was nothing more than business on the grandest scale of all. He tucked Cinnamon Cartier's file under his arm and headed for his office. A woman, young, beautiful and intelligent. An unknown, walking in and showing the big boys how it was done. He liked it. It took guts to tackle the Establishment. He had always admired courage. Jonathon wanted him to get close to Cinnamon. Well, his boss would get his wish.

"What do you think, Cinnamon? How did we sound?"

"Fantastic, as usual, Linda." Cinnamon rose from the chair behind the desk and crossed the study of the Metcalf home. The quiet, book-lined room was her favorite in the country-style house. She smiled at the petite, dark-haired wife of her boss. "The dress was just right." She turned, including the twins in her praise. "You boys were great. You had every girl's eye between the ages of thirteen and twenty."

"Don't tell them that, Cinnamon. You're just feeding their already oversized egos." Donald Metcalf spoke as he entered, a wide grin stretched across his handsome face as he hugged his wife and clapped his sons on the back. The four could have starred in a commercial for family of the year: pretty, adoring wife; tall, blond husband, and sons the image of their father. The loving circle could have been publicity hype, but it wasn't. In this era of public figures being less than what they appeared, the Metcalfs were very rare.

"I think I'm going to start calling you the 'dynamite quad.' If I win the election it's going to be because of the four of you." His smile encompassed Cinnamon, even though she carefully stood outside the family circle.

Linda looked at her husband, pride and love vivid in her expression. "Actually I think Cinnamon should get the lion's share of the credit. She picked my dress, coached me on what to say to those reporters and made sure I even had the mannerisms down pat." She laughed a little as she said the last. "How she ever knew what they would ask, almost down to the last comma, I'll never know."

"Street smarts," Gary, the elder twin by ten minutes, murmured. "I heard one of the reporters talking about you and Dad today. He said Pop was one lucky guy to have a campaign worker with the legs and body of a call girl and the mind of a political general."

"Gary!" Linda stared at her son with shocked eyes.

"I think you owe Cinnamon an apology, son," Donald said firmly.

Cinnamon laughed softly. Her tender sensibilities had toughened up long ago. She had heard worse from people being far less than complimentary. "Forget it. I've been called worse."

Gary reddened. "I thought it was a compliment. She is beautiful." His voice cracked on the words, but he managed to stare at his idol without blushing. His brother nodded, looking only slightly less moon-struck.

Cinnamon blinked, her amusement dying. She had been so caught up in her work that she had missed the near-adoration building in the younger Metcalfs. She remembered too well the tender psyche of an adoles-cent. How many times had she been pushed aside be-cause she wasn't pretty enough, smart enough or old enough.

"Well, actually, guys, I think it was a compliment. I think you just startled your parents with how grown-up you're becoming." She grinned at them. "Parents aren't used to their boys talking about call girls and political generals in the same breath."

The twins exchanged looks, then grinned wickedly. "They've got worse on TV and those aren't even the shows they have to edit for kids."

Cinnamon glanced at Linda and Don. Their expressions were clearing, the smiles reigning again. The tour had been hard on them all. Too little sleep, too many towns, no privacy and more nosey, some-times ugly, questions than anyone wanted to answer. Everyone was holding up well as far as the media could see. But here, behind closed doors, innocent words that would have been laughed off a few weeks ago took on new meaning. The smiles were strained, the eyes shadowed with weariness, the shoulders less square, the movements not nearly so energetic. The price of success. She was even more glad that she had been able to schedule a one-week break for the Metcalfs before they had to hit the campaign trail in earnest, preparing for the New Hampshire primary.

"How would you like seven whole days just for us?" Don asked, glancing down at his wife.

. Linda brightened, looking back at him. "You mean it? One whole week?"

He nodded before kissing her gently. "I told Cinnamon we needed a break and then left her to find a way to make sure we got one. As usual, she came through."

Linda reached out and caught Cinnamon's hand. "I don't know what we would do without you."

Ben sat back in his chair and stared at the blank TV screen as the VCR rewound the tape on Cinnamon Cartier. He decided to view it again. Jonathon hadn't exaggerated the woman's influence on the Metcalfs. Every one of them was clearly under her spell. He pushed the play button and popped the top on the soft drink at his elbow. Her face stared at him before he finished the first swallow.

The scene was a press conference with Donald Metcalf, his wife Linda, their twins, Gary and Mark, flanking them. Cinnamon stood to the right and off to one side. All four Metcalfs had a clear view of her. Reporters shouted questions. Flashbulbs flashed and through it all, the four on the dais moved so that they presented a beautifully proportioned shot of the American family. The smiles they exchanged carried just the right touch of caring and intimacy. The boys with their budding golden Beach Boy images were probably pumping up every young female's viewers' blood pressure and hormone levels. Metcalf answered his questions with seeming ease and sincerity.

Linda did her part with a kind of sweet, I-love-my-husband-and-he's-the-best-for-the-job replies.

If Jonathon hadn't warned him, Ben might have been so taken in by the fairy-tale look at the Metcalfs to miss the subtle signals Cinnamon gave. He had seen football coaches handle their teams from the sidelines with less finesse. The woman was extraordinary. With a lift of a brow, she warned Metcalf to evade a direct answer. With a touch of a finger to her temple, she corrected the too-devilish grins of the twins. With a slight inclination of her chin, she commanded a stronger posture from Linda Metcalf when only a second before she had been leaning against her husband as though she were tired.

"Woman, you are really good. No wonder Jonathon is worried. You scare me and I'm just sitting here watching you."

The more he studied her, the more signals he saw. That would have been bad enough, but seeing the complete detachment of her gaze hit him hard. Those people were nothing more than players to her. Every one of them was dancing to her tune and they didn't even know it. His eyes narrowed, concentrating on Cinnamon. Where was her weakness? Everyone had one. He was still womanizing, five play throughs later. He was still without an answer.

"Damn!"

Ben rewound the tape and glared at the machine. The dossier lay on the table beside him. Reaching for the phone he dialed Jonathon's home number. It was after midnight and he knew Jonathon wasn't going to be happy at being awakened, but he didn't care. A grumpy voice answered.

"Do you know what time it is?"

Ben ignored the demand. "Are you having her followed?"

"Yes, but it didn't do a bit of good. She is rarely alone and when she isn't, she's with one of the Metcalfs."

"No man in her life?"

"The senator, probably, but they're so discreet we can't prove it."

"I thought you said his wife always traveled with him."

"She does. So what?"

Ben frowned deeply, not liking the disgust he felt to think that Cinnamon Cartier was sleeping with Metcalf while his wife was close by. On second thought, he didn't like the idea of her sleeping with the man at all.

"Anything else you want to know? Or can I go back to sleep now?" Jonathon demanded testily.

"Into each life a little rain must fall," Ben muttered before hanging up on Jonathon's irritable response.

He ran the tape again. This time he looked for any betrayal of a physical relationship between Metcalf and Cinnamon. There wasn't one. Leaning back in his chair, he studied her image where he had frozen it on the scene.

Her eyes. Dark, deep and disillusioned. Her secrets were there. Whoever she was, she hadn't become Cinnamon Cartier by accident; nor had she reached her last birthday without more than one trial by fire. If she believed in or trusted anyone or anything, then he would go out and buy a hat so that he could eat it. His hands clenched into fists as he sat there staring at her. There was a tiny scar between her brow and her hairline on the left side of her face. Another woman might have tried to hide the blemish either with a hairstyle or cosmetics. Cinnamon had done neither. Nor had she flaunted the mark. Instead, she seemed not to care that it was there. Yet this same woman took such attention to detail where her puppets were concerned. He had no doubt, now, just how much influence she wielded with the Metcalfs.

"Two days, lonely lady. Then we shall see what we both are. Will you be taken in by my camouflage or will you see through me as I have you?"

CHLOE THE STUDY

Two

The travel alarm buzzed insistently. Cinnamon reached out and slapped it off without opening her eyes. Six o'clock. Most people would have considered it an indecent hour. But then most people didn't have her hectic kind of life or almost total lack of privacy. Opening her eyes, she stretched and slipped from the bed. The semidarkness of the room cloaked her nakedness in shadows but didn't disguise the unusual fitness of her body. The whistle-bait figure was no accident, nor was the almost silent way she moved. Taking a mat from the closet across the room, she placed it on the floor to face the window. Opening the outer drapes, but leaving the sheers drawn for privacy, she stared out at the predawn sky. Ten deep breaths, slow and easy, then she took her place on the yoga mat. Assuming a lotus position she began her morning ritual of exercise and meditation. It was over an hour later before she surfaced to start her day.

The phone rang as she was finishing breakfast. A quick glance at the clock showed just past eight.

"Cinnamon, I need you to talk to you. Something odd has happened. It may not mean anything. And then again, it might."

The puzzlement in Don's voice was unusual enough to get Cinnamon's full attention. "Do you want me to come over?"

"I wish you would. I almost didn't call you, because the whole idea sounded so farfetched."

His words trailed off into an awkward silence that increased Cinnamon's uneasiness. "Half an hour, tops," she promised before hanging up.

Donald and Linda were waiting for her in the living room when she arrived at their home. "What's up?" She took the chair facing them. The tension and worry in their expressions spoke of more than just an ordinary problem.

"You know we went out to dinner last night?"

She nodded. The question was odd, since it was her job to set up their itinerary.

"We haven't had much time with the boys, so we took them with us. You know how they are. Never still for a minute. After dinner they wandered around a bit. Linda and I didn't pay much attention. When we got home they acted a little strange, but again we didn't notice all that much. This morning we found out they overheard a rather strange conversation at the restaurant."

Linda sat forward. "They heard two men talking downstairs when they were waiting for the elevator. Someone is having us followed. I can't believe it. I knew that every little thing we do is possible public fodder, but I never expected to be followed. I didn't think it could happen in this country."

"That's not exactly what the boys said," Donald interrupted, covering her hands with his. "What they heard was that the two were there to keep watch for you, Cinnamon."

Cinnamon thought swiftly while staring at the Metcalfs without really seeing them. She knew they were waiting for reassurance. When she had first begun to work for Donald, she had realized how she enjoyed the political arena, how she had a flair for that kind of life. To realize a dream, she had taken a calculated risk, by becoming important to the senator. Never expecting to be thrust into the full view of the country in a presidential race. She had meant to stay on the fringes of the political scene, but her intentions had not been able to control circumstances. Donald had announced his determination to try for the presidential nomination. She had to either lose her dream to make something of herself, take a chance at getting another place with another politician or take an even greater risk by staying put. After much soul-searching she had stayed, deciding that the best place to hide something could be in plain sight. Her cover had carried her this far. With luck, planning and care, it might just take her into the White House.

"Do you know why they would be following you?" Donald asked when she didn't answer.

Cinnamon smiled a little—a gesture to reassure. "I'm the new kid on the block. We all are. We're close to pulling off the impossible. We're worrying the big guys. You and Linda are safe because you're living the truth. Logically, I'm the next target. You can't fight an enemy you don't know.''

Donald's face darkened with anger. "That doesn't make it right. You don't even sound surprised or worried.''

Cinnamon's smile widened naturally. Don was one of the good guys all the way through. "I'm worried all right but there's no point in making a federal case out of it. Whoever's put the tail on me, as the TV cops would say, is going to keep on until he either finds what he's looking for or realizes there isn't anything there to find and gives up. I can't do anything in either case.'' She paused, her amusement dying. "But you can. You can send me packing.''

"What?'' Donald surged to his feet.

"Cinnamon, you can't mean it.'' Linda was right behind him.

They had given her a chance that no one else would have, when she had been all determination and had had precious little experience. She didn't want to see them hurt. She knew the risks. She could live with losing and starting over again. They couldn't. "You should think about it. Whoever our friend is he wouldn't try something like this unless he believed he had cause.''

The warning was as close as she would come to the truth. She liked the Metcalfs, cared for them as much as she was able to care for anyone. She would ride their coattails up the ladder of success, building the ladder with her own two hands when the need arose, but she had never shared who she really was with anyone.

Donald stared at her intently. "Is there something that we should know about?" he asked after a moment.

Linda glared at him. "What a question, Don. Cinnamon's our friend. She's been with us for eight years now. Worked as a runner, organizer, fund raiser. Your secretary. She was the one who helped me with the twins when they had the mumps that time while you were snowed in Bristol. Now she's your assistant, your campaign manager. She's done more for us than anyone else. Every dream you have she helped us get."

Cinnamon felt like squirming in her chair. Linda didn't know how carefully she had selected the candidate to work for that very first year; didn't know how carefully she had studied every aide's style and his success-and-failure rate, the candidates he'd backed, and why. Linda couldn't know about the computer whiz she'd dated for three months who had taught her how to use a machine to project election results, campaign directions and platforms; or the psych major who had been her best friend, the one who had taught her the meaning and value of the spoken word and body language. Every part of her life was a piece carefully selected to fit the whole.

"Don's right."

"No, he's not." Linda turned her glare on Cinnamon.

Donald sighed and ran a hand through his hair. "I'm sorry. This campaign has put me on edge. Someone with your kind of ambition wouldn't set themselves up without knowing exactly what you were doing. I should have remembered that. You can forget about leaving. We're in this together, no matter what."

Cinnamon rose, studying him. "You're sure." He was far less naive than his wife. It would be harder to hide from him than some hired detective without the spur of a personal stake in the outcome.

"Positive." He gestured toward the coffee maker on the table in front of him. "Now let's talk about something else. As you say, we can't change your shadows."

Cinnamon didn't blink at the double meaning of his last words. Too many years had gone into training herself not to react unless she deliberately chose to. Turning, she reached into her briefcase and extracted an appointment sheet. All of the time slots were full.

"You have an impromptu press conference at ten."

Linda laughed softly, settling on the couch again. "I never have been able to figure how you can plan an impromptu conference," she murmured, clearly glad the storm was past.

"Simple. An anonymous call to the biggest paper in town usually does the trick. Here in Washington, it's a tad bit more difficult. People here are more distrustful and mercenary."

Linda poured them all coffee.

"At eleven-thirty Don and I are due at lunch with the minority whip. We should finish by three. Then it's back here to change and pick you up, Linda, for the Daytons' dinner. We should get back around one tomorrow morning."

"We hope," Donald put in dryly. "What about tomorrow?"

"One radio interview, and that's it except for the fund-raiser dinner."

"Then we can go home to Tennessee for a while." Linda leaned back sipping her coffee. "I can hardly wait. It seems like years instead of weeks since we hit the campaign trail.''

"And you've been a trooper.'' Donald leaned back, so that he could kiss his wife. "I couldn't have done half as well without you. You charm everyone.''

"I'll second that.'' Cinnamon raised her cup in sincere salute.

Linda smiled in delight before lifting her own cup. "To all of us.''

Ben watched Metcalf come out of the office building with Cinnamon walking beside him. A small army of reporters swarmed near the entrance, orchestrated, no doubt, by Ms. Cartier, he decided cynically as he watched her take a step back so it seemed that the senator was the only one of importance present. The questions were shouted in rapid succession. Through it all, Cinnamon remained in the background, her eyes on Metcalf. Ben studied her closely, wanting to find something about her that didn't appeal to him. The sun in her hair showed rich red highlights. The cut of her dark blue two-piece suit displayed a figure that was even more impressive in real life than it had been on videotape. Yet it was her stillness that intrigued him now. In the sea of mostly male faces, in the chaos of so many people talking at once, she stood silently as though alone. Her expression remained detached. Even her hands, which usually betrayed the nervous or untrained, were relaxed and quiet.

"Baby, you are really good,'' he murmured.

As if she had heard him speak, her head turned, and her eyes found his. Those eyes. Even with the few yards that separated them he could see that same look that was in every photo, every frame of the videotape. The hunted: the wary animal that man would watch well. The relaxation left her body. He felt rather than saw the change. The chin inched up a fraction. Testing the wind. Sending a challenge. His gaze sharpened. What had she sensed, he wondered, knowing that nothing in his appearance should have alerted her. He had on his most nondescript jacket, slightly scuffed loafers and his favorite blue slacks. He should have been projecting the image of a slightly bored sightseer, with a landmark brochure tucked in his pocket and a camera slung over one arm. The hat he wore shaded a good deal of his face and the slightly slouched position he had taken disguised his height and build. Yet she had picked him out as if he wore a sign. Damn and double damn!

Cinnamon turned her head away from the man standing on the edge of the crowd. It took a surprising amount of concentration to focus on the questions still being tossed at Don. She wanted to look back at the man. More than that, she wanted to demand to know why he was studying her like a bug under a microscope. Her reaction was odd since she didn't know why she thought she had so much of his attention, nor did she believe he was a tourist. Instinct guided her. Reflexes learned on the street had given her an uncanny ability to see what others did not. Those same reflexes had been invaluable in the campaign, but not once had they whispered a warning to her personally, as they did now.

The time for that kind of protection was over, or so she had believed until recently. Was this one of the men following her? A careful glance at her watch told her it was time to free Don from his audience. Slipping between reporters, she touched his arm, fielding the last question herself.

"No, we have no idea what the minority whip wishes to see us about and it would be very inappropriate for us to guess." She smiled as she offered the rebuke.

"Very inappropriate," Donald added, making his way to the waiting limousine.

"Ms. Cartier, one more question." A woman thrust a mike under Cinnamon's nose.

Cinnamon stopped, giving Don a look to indicate she would enter the car last.

Ben noted the exchange.

"It's been said that you must have some family connections or at least some history in the political arena, yet you have gone on record denying either. How do you account for your ability to play the big boys' game?"

Cinnamon met the sharp eyes of Nola Winters. She didn't like the woman's abrasive style but she couldn't help admiring her brain and her grit in the way she went after a story.

"Luck," she murmured with a smile that wasn't intended to fool anyone. "That's what our opponents say. Along with the charge that we'll fold in the stretch. Speed but no staying power I believe is the assessment." She glanced over the heads of her audience, her eyes finding her possible shadow once more. The sun was to his back. She could see nothing of his features but it didn't matter. His presence was enough to hold her attention.

"It will be interesting to discover if they're right." Maybe it was impulse that made her give the tiniest tip of her head. Maybe it was sheer recklessness. Whatever it was, she felt imminently satisfied to see the faint stiffening of his back before he turned and walked away. The exchange only took a second. No one noticed. With a smile and a shake of her head for the last questions tossed her way, Cinnamon got into the limo beside Don. Immediately, the door shut, giving some relief to the confusion outside.

"It's either getting easier by the day or else those reporters are beginning to ease up on us," Don remarked, relaxing in the seat.

Cinnamon followed suit. "Probably a little bit of both. We're getting past the nine day wonder stage. The race is heating up. We're gaining in the polls and people are starting to take you seriously."

Don looked at her curiously. "Don't you ever get excited or nervous? I think I spend a lot of my time that way."

She smiled slightly. "Not often. No time."

"I'm working you too hard."

"No harder than I wish to work." The truth slipped out but she didn't try to disguise it. "I like working. I like reaching for the improbable and the impossible. Haven't you noticed how sweet those kind of victories are?"

Don shook his head. "Sometimes you sound so driven. No matter how much I want this election, I can't quite get that same intensity. Sometimes I wonder if you shouldn't be the one running instead of me. You'd make a good president. You're unflappable, quick, intelligent and you can talk on any subject at the drop of a hat."

Few things struck Cinnamon as truly funny. This one did. "This country isn't ready for that kind of shock yet," she said, laughing softly. "Besides

Madam President Cinnamon Cartier doesn't sound quite right. No pomp, no solid sound of reliability. My name would make better billing for a stripper."

It was Don's turn to laugh. "Maybe you could change your name," he suggested.

Cinnamon pretended to consider. The conversation was silly, but if it helped Donald relax for the upcoming meeting with the minority whip, then she was willing to go along with the game. Don had so many good points both as a politician and a man. His attention to detail, his true caring for the country. His solid, if not inspired thinking might not set the world on fire, but it would be a pillar of common sense. But what really impressed Cinnamon was his dedication. That was the reason she had aligned herself with his campaign. She could not have worked for a man she did not admire and respect. One lie in her life was all that she intended to tolerate.

"How about Ellen Smith?" she asked.

Don blinked, then chuckled deeply. "You've got to be kidding! You don't look like an Ellen Smith. Ellen Smiths bake cookies, go to PTO meetings, drive car pools, teach or become secretaries. Wonderful, hardworking women in their own way but not the kind to take on a campaign, handle hostile reporters or plan strategy."

"It's a good thing I know you don't mean that, or I'd throw you to your detractors with a smile on my face. Talk about prejudicial statements...."

He held up his hand in surrender. "Do you think you look like an Ellen Smith?"

"No, but then I don't think I look like a Cinnamon Cartier, either." She shrugged, momentarily wishing she had never allowed the conversation to get this far.

She had thought she had trained her need to play with fire out of her system. Maybe spending eight years in her new identity had made her complacent, prone to take unnecessary chances. Glancing out the window she saw with relief that they had reached their destination.

The restaurant was one of the best in the city, as well-known for its clientele as it was for its cuisine. Together, Cinnamon and Don crossed the elegantly appointed interior to the booth set by the windows. The minority whip, Samuel Reed, was already seated.

"You've really done a good job with our man here. The polls are showing impressive gains." Sam Reed's shrewd eyes weighed Cinnamon up.

Cinnamon met the assessment with one of her own. This man could make or break them with the party. A whip wielded that kind of power. "We have a fine organization."

"Good enough to gain a three-point rise in the polls in this pre preliminary campaigning. I'll be really interested to see how you do in New Hampshire. With our party being the minority, there are quite a number of candidates who think they can put us back on the political map." The cynicism in his words was blatant.

"Everyone likes to believe his man is the best."

"Do you?"

A challenge. "Would I be pushing so hard if I didn't?" Counter thrust. His surprise was quickly veiled.

Donald sat back, knowing that this testing had little to do with him at the moment.

"You came out of nowhere."

"That bothers a lot of people. Always better the devil you know than the one you don't."

"Tell me about yourself."

"I'm sure your grapevine has given you everything up to and including my shoe size, but I'll repeat it if you like."

His brows rose, a faint admiration flickering. "You live up to your reputation," he murmured finally, glancing at Don.

"Tough, streetwise and stubborn." She smiled slightly as she quoted the more often repeated charges against her. "I would have gone under by now if I weren't."

"True." Sam sat back as their waiter brought their food.

Talk was general while they ate. Party platform, Don's thoughts on the upcoming primary, the impossibility of relaxing one's guard around the media and the problems of running a full-fledged campaign while still functioning as an active member of the Senate.

Cinnamon listened to every word, not really expecting any difficulties between Sam and Don, but feeling equally unwilling to take any chances. About halfway through the meal, she felt as though someone were watching her with more than ordinary interest. Discreetly glancing around, she tried to see if her shadow had followed her into the restaurant. She found nothing unusual in any of the other patrons. Whoever was watching her was well hidden. That thought was not reassuring.

Ben wondered what had alerted Cinnamon. He saw her stiffen, angle her head to scan the other diners. How had she known he was there? Was it possible that someone had tipped her off to his presence? And yet she hadn't spotted him, despite the careful looks around she took every few minutes. Intrigued, irritated and curious, Ben sat through his meal, watching Cinnamon and hardly doing justice to his prime rib. When he had decided to follow the woman he had given himself a dozen reasons why it was necessary. Her two tails had turned up nothing. Jonathon had taken them off the case. It was unlikely he would find anything either this way. And yet here he sat.

She lifted her head again, the light turning her hair to fire. Ben inhaled sharply, feeling the slam of desire in his midsection. He hadn't been affected this strongly by the sight of a woman since he'd been a teenager. He wasn't supposed to feel anything for Cinnamon Cartier beyond the confines of his job. He swore silently.

Her face turned, the sun from the window highlighting the clean line of her jaw, the mouth that seldom smiled and those eyes so filled with secrets. She was looking straight at him. He had chosen his table deliberately, wanting the shadowed alcove to screen him from possible detection. She should be able to see his outline, but nothing else while he could look his fill.

"Beautiful," he muttered almost angrily as she turned back to her companions. His hands clenched around the knife and fork, stifling his urge to get up and go to her; to snatch her away from the two men who held most of her attention. Was she sleeping with Donald Metcalf? The question haunted him.

He waited until the three made their departure before taking his leave. Tomorrow at the fund-raiser would be their first face-to-face meeting. His anticipation was annoying and worrying. He didn't want to believe she was guilty of anything. How far would he have to go to get the information they needed? The question had never bothered him before. Now he couldn't escape the demand. Disgusted with himself for being hooked in by Jonathon, he walked part of the way to the office, hoping to work off some of his temper. It was bad luck that the secretary Jonathon had loaned him had taken a message from his boss.

"He wants to see you as soon as you come in."

He swore. He wasn't normally given to turning the air blue but he was fast developing the habit.

Her smile was sympathetic. "Tough day?"

"You don't know the half of it." He rested one hip on the edge of his desk. "I think I'm getting too old for this business," he muttered.

Startled, Sharon looked at him curiously. "That doesn't sound like you at all. It must have been one wicked day." She gestured to the littered desk and chaotic files. "I would switch jobs with you, but I'd probably fall over my own feet."

"You wouldn't like the work. Better to stick to this place. At least you get a decent place to eat and can sleep in your own place when the mood strikes." Ben pushed himself erect. It wasn't like him to complain. The closer he came to getting out of the business, the more he realized he had made the right decision. Sighing wearily, he made his way to Jonathon's office.

"Tell me that expression means you've found something."

"It doesn't." Ben dropped into the chair and glared at his boss. "You've had more than a month to turn up something. Don't expect me to turn up a miracle almost overnight."

Jonathon sighed wearily. "I'm getting heat from upstairs. Ms. Cartier is really making some people nervous."

"She ought to. The woman is good—maybe the best I've ever seen."

Jonathon frowned heavily. "Just what does that mean?"

"It means that she's more than smart. She's quick and alert. Catching her at anything is going to be worse than tough. She isn't going to be stampeded into making mistakes and I doubt she'll make any on her own."

"I can't believe Apollo is stumped. You've still got the party tomorrow night."

Ben wanted to walk out. The implication was obvious and repellent. There had been a time when he wouldn't have thought so. Maybe it was that this time, no one was sure that Cinnamon Cartier was really a threat. Or maybe he was getting too old and too jaded for the game. Better either explanation than the belief that the woman herself was responsible for his wish to be out of the situation. To be drawn to her, to have her in his mind to such a degree that it disturbed his sleep was irritating. Now she was making him question the course of his life, the choices he had made for his country and the strategies he had employed.

"Don't worry. I'll do this last job right." Ben pushed to his feet, feeling every one of his thirty-eight years. "If she's into what you seem to think, I'll nail her for you."

Three

_____

Cinnamon returned to her apartment, barely closing the door behind her before she started stepping out of her clothes. She was late again, as usual. No matter how carefully she allotted her time, there always seemed to be something on the horizon designed to throw her off schedule. This time it had been drinks and a short chat with the chief of the Washington campaign office. Of course, the man had had more on his mind than just politics. She grimaced as she stepped into the shower. It wasn't the first time a male had thought she would be willing to "put out" to further Don's career. She was well aware that it was whispered that she and Don were more than just business associates.

At first the idea had amused her. If she were to take a man into her life, it wouldn't be one like Don. Solid reliability and softness were wonderful characteristics for some women, but not for her. She needed strength and power in a mate; a man to challenge her and keep her on her toes. Don couldn't keep a pussycat on its toes if he tried. Linda was just the right wife for him.

As for her, she wasn't ready to commit herself to a relationship. She still had a long way to go in building her career. Don was just the rung on the ladder. She'd make a name for herself whether he won or lost.

Cinnamon knew the power bosses were beginning to take a serious look at her. In big-government politics, her sex was against her. But she was determined to beat the odds. So far, she had won more than she had lost. Adrenaline flowed as she thought of the New Hampshire primary coming up in a few weeks. Don and Linda would have a week to rest and relax beforehand, but she was only taking tomorrow and the weekend. There was still so much to do; so much she could accomplish. She wanted Don to win. Badly. She believed in his ability to do the job.

Her past—the time before Cinnamon Cartier was "born"—could have, perhaps *should* have, taken a toll on her scruples. She had gone hungry, been wet, cold and tired because of her conscience. Keeping the wolves from the door, food in her belly and ultimately knowledge in her mind had made her bend the rules once. She had never forgotten the feeling of guilt, nor had she ever ceased to regret what she had had to do to survive.

Cinnamon might have the reputation for being sharp and maybe a bit loose with the senator, but she had done nothing anyone could point a finger at. Not so with Ellen Smith. Don had thought she'd picked a name out of a hat. It had been picked out of a hat, all right, but not by her. The bitter thought was disturbing. She frowned, realizing she was wasting precious time on things that no hand on earth could change. The past was done. She had seen to that. No one would ever connect Ellen Smith and Cinnamon Cartier.

Stepping out of the shower, she toweled dry vigorously before walking into the bedroom and pulling a slim black dress out of the small closet. The silk swathe looked like nothing on the hanger. Wearing it was a different matter. The fluid fabric clung in all the right places and yet still managed to convey an elegant, understated image—just the right note for a money seeking black-tie dinner. Most of the women there tonight would be vying for the title of "best dressed" in attendance. The last thing she wanted to do was to antagonize a potential contributor by upstaging his wife or mistress. Discreet sapphire studs and lightly applied makeup completed the picture. The clock showed that she wouldn't be late, after all. The limo should be just pulling up downstairs. The phone rang. It was Linda.

"We're ready. Are you?"

"On the dot," Cinnamon replied, her tone unconsciously soft. Normally her husky voice was decisive, leaving no room for argument. But with Linda she tempered her personality so the older woman wouldn't be overwhelmed. Despite the difference in their ages, Linda was by far the less self-assured.

"The limo and I will be with you in a half hour."

The estate where the dinner was given was ablaze with lights. Valets in scarlet coats moved swiftly between cars helping ladies out, moving vehicles and creating order out of what could have been chaos.

Many of Washington's trendsetters were attending. When Donald had taken the heart of the public as the soft-spoken, sincere young Southerner who spoke of a return to the values of the strong America past, Washington society had opened its pocketbook and its doors. All that could change tomorrow. Cinnamon mounted the stairs, a faintly cynical smile on her lips. One wrong word, one important person snubbed, angered or humiliated, and Donald could be as politically dead as a three-day-old fish. Politics was a tough game, not for the fainthearted or the squeamish.

"Senator, Mrs. Metcalf, Ms. Cartier." Their host greeted them as long-lost friends.

Cinnamon's smile deepened. The man hadn't met Don until tonight. She had handled all the arrangements. She lifted a glass of wine off a tray carried by a passing waiter. As Don and Linda began to circulate in one direction she took the other. They would keep an eye on each other, ready to join forces should the need arise. But otherwise, they'd act as two separate factions.

Ben watched Cinnamon move from group to group. The change that overtook her as she approached each gathering was subtle yet distinct. No matter what the conversational climate, she seemed to charge her audience with curiosity and adrenaline, making them act as though they were privileged to be in on something extraordinary. His admiration went up a notch, especially when he noticed that the women received exactly the same care and attention as the men. She could have used her sex—there were certainly enough signals being tossed her way. But she didn't. She seemed to ignore those messages, yet he could tell she was completely aware of the atmosphere.

Her glass was empty, he noted. He signaled a waiter and murmured his order. A few minutes later the man reappeared bearing two unusual drinks. Despite the press of people between them, he reached her side in a moment. The group around her dispersed easily, clearly done with their chat. Ben decided he was well satisfied with his timing. As he approached her, he inhaled deeply of her scent as it swirled softly about him. Exotic, earthy, and yet it was so light it teased rather than overwhelmed the senses. He touched her arm lightly, a smile hovering on his lips as he wondered what the next few minutes would bring.

"Your drink."

The feel of a man's hand on her arm and then the slow, drawling voice near her ear startled Cinnamon. Turning her head, she found herself looking up into the sleepiest eyes she had ever seen. The fact that she had to look up at all was a novelty for a woman who stood five-foot-eleven in her high heels. The next surprise was the face that went with the sleepy eyes was smiling at her yet there was nothing of a man on the make in his expression. Intrigued when she shouldn't have been, Cinnamon looked closer only to be diverted by the feel of icy glass pressed into her hand.

"You looked thirsty. I think you'll like this."

Cinnamon stared at the pale pink liquid. "What is it?"

"A Bellini. Not everyone likes them. Peaches and champagne. You looked like a woman who might appreciate the combination."

Cinnamon lifted the glass and took a sip.

"You aren't afraid of trying things. I like that," Ben murmured, watching her.

Cinnamon tipped her head, studying him. "Meaning?"

"You didn't take a cautious taste. Most people would have."

"Don't you mean most women?"

"If I had, I would have said so." He slipped a hand beneath her elbow and guided her toward the terrace. "I've been watching you work this mob. You're good. No wonder Metcalf thinks so highly of you."

Cinnamon let him lead her out in the darkness. She knew if she stood alone at the party it wouldn't be long before someone sought her out. Anyway, she was in need of a break, she decided silently. It was too bad it wasn't the only one. She was curious and interested. The drink line wasn't a new one, but the lack of a follow-up either in words or expression was. Most men complimented the woman not the person.

"You have the advantage of me," she murmured as she turned and leaned against the rail, watching him.

"Benjamin Forsythe. Benjamin, or Ben to my friends."

He propped his shoulder against a column and sipped his drink, deciding that her eyes were even more extraordinary up close: darker, deeper and more secretive. She had a voice that made a man lean closer to catch every syllable, and a figure that, even shrouded in black, was eye riveting. Dynamite in a living package—and he was feeling like a lit fuse. If he didn't start thinking about the job and not the woman he would need an ice-cube bath to put out the fire.

"Cinnamon Cartier. I think I prefer Ben to Benjamin. Do you mind?"

"I know who you are and, no, I don't mind you calling me Ben."

The faint emphasis she heard on the *you* was unmistakable and telling. Here comes the pass. The disappointment she felt surprised her.

"How do you know what to say to every person you speak to? Or is it the same spiel?"

Cinnamon blinked, again thrown off guard. "I don't know what you mean." The comment was meant to gain her thinking time. It also got her a flicker of disappointment in his sleepy eyes. Cinnamon felt oddly guilty without knowing why. "I don't use spiels."

Ben shrugged. "Campaigning then. A more acceptable word, perhaps."

She recognized the cynicism in his voice. "You don't approve of this."

"I don't disapprove. Besides, I'm here, am I not?"

Cinnamon had never liked games where she didn't know the rules. "Many possible explanations."

"Perhaps I'm following you." Shock often achieved what planning did not. But not this time.

"Are you?" She held his gaze steadily. He didn't look the type to spy on others. He had the contented mien of a professor or a man of books. He didn't look at all like the type to put himself out to follow anyone. And yet her gaze sharpened—instincts that never truly slept tingling.

Ben saw the change only because he was watching for it. "Yes and no. I came alone tonight. Nothing worse than one of these things without someone along to break up the monotony. I was beginning to get bored and when I get bored I get sleepy. Not good manners to snore in the middle of a black-tie affair. Might drown in the champagne punch to boot."

He laughed at himself and at the lie. In truth he was a people watcher and always had been. Parties amused him simply because the creatures who attended had more antics than the monkeys at the National Zoo.

"I don't think I believe that," Cinnamon said slowly.

Ben took the empty glass from her hand and set it with his on the table beside them. The action kept his hands busy and his arms empty. He had her intrigued. He wanted to keep her that way.

"What would you believe?"

Frustrated, Cinnamon shook her head. "I don't know."

"I haven't come on like gangbusters, although you are probably the most sexy woman I've ever seen. You give me ideas that would get me arrested." He laughed, genuinely amused when she glared at him. "You didn't like the first answer," he pointed out.

"There was no reason for that."

"I couldn't resist."

"Did you think I expected it?" The thought made her angry.

Her anger doused his humor. He risked reaching out to touch her cheek, and was not surprised when she pulled back before he could make contact. This woman was not into casually given signs of affection, or even interest.

"No. I had hoped to make you smile."

Oddly enough, she wanted to believe him. She decided she should be back inside. From the noise spilling into the darkness, she could tell things were in full swing. She should be working and yet she couldn't make herself move. It was pleasant, relaxing, to stand in the shadows with Ben and talk of nothing. The tension in her body that only yoga had ever had the power to release eased.

"Would you like to try again?"

Ben almost regretted the softening he sensed in her. He had tricked her. He knew it was necessary, but this time he didn't like his part.

"Not now. You're on your guard. It will be much better if I catch you unawares."

"Cinnamon, are you busy?"

Don's voice drew Cinnamon's attention. She stifled a feeling of regret at the intrusion.

"Break time's over," Ben said as he stepped back.

Cinnamon turned her head to answer Don. "I'll be right in." When she turned back to Ben, she discovered she was alone on the terrace. She glanced at the table. Even the glasses were gone. Don was waiting. She moved out of the shadows and into the light, noise and energy of her real life. The man and the moments on the terrace didn't fit.

Knowing that didn't stop her from looking around for Ben, but he was nowhere to be seen. Annoyed with herself for caring, she tried to focus on the various people vying for her attention. She managed, but it was difficult. And that only increased her irritation with herself. By the time the party was drawing to a close, she was in no mood for another supporter questioning her on Don's chances and how the campaign was really shaping up. This man was a heavy contributor so she forced herself to listen even when she saw Don and Linda leave the room. It was late, she was tired. One of her very rare headaches was starting to build. Suddenly, the man stopped speaking, a grin lighting his expression.

"Only for you would I have done this, Benny."

"Thanks, Kyle. I owe you one."

Cinnamon turned at the sound of his voice, not noticing Kyle slipping away.

"Just who are you?" Cinnamon demanded, recognizing a setup when she saw one. "And what do you owe Kyle Richards?"

"A favor for keeping you busy while the senator and his wife left in the limo."

"That much I figured out. I just wondered how much a trick like that would be worth."

Ben accepted her anger. "I wanted to take you home. I stacked the cards in my favor."

Her gaze sharpened at the easy explanation. "Why?"

He laughed, liking her claws and her caution. "Why do you think?"

"You don't seem the type."

"Why? Because I didn't make a pass at you on the terrace? Because I didn't tell you I like you in black? That hair the color of rich wine appeals to me more than any other? That your skin feels as silky as that little bit of nothing you're wearing? That I applaud your taste in clothes when you're working? Would you have listened? You've been fending off passes all night. Some subtle, and a few not so subtle. Why be one of a crowd?"

"Well, you definitely are different with this kind of a stunt," she murmured, torn between glaring at him and smiling.

"You can call a cab. I'll even pay the bill, since I'm the one who stranded you."

"Now that's what I call nice strategy." Her admiration was real. "You've got a light hand with the advance-and-retreat technique."

He tipped his head, enjoying himself more with each conversational thrust. "You're good yourself."

She shrugged. "I have to be."

He let that pass. "So what's your decision? May I drive you home? Or will you condemn me to loneliness?"

"Home is an apartment across town. Probably out of your way. And I don't know you."

Ben nodded, having expected the answer. In field-work he had learned to rely on his instincts. He would get no closer if he didn't give her a reason to trust him. "I'm with security around here," he murmured, keeping his reply vague. "Here, I'll even show you my ID. Does that satisfy you?"

This time she did glare at him. It wasn't difficult to believe his occupation. He had the kind of face a person could depend on, perhaps even trust. "A gentleman wouldn't keep pushing."

"I never said I was a gentleman. Your boss is but I'm not." Harshness crept into his tone before he could stop it.

Cinnamon stepped back, understanding that he referred to the half-formed belief of the rumor circulating about her and Don. "That was definitely an error in tactics." She reached for her handbag, which was lying on the sofa beside her. "I'll pay for my own cab."

Ben caught her hand before she could slip out of his reach. "I apologize."

She glanced down to the surprisingly callused fingers encircling her wrist. The strength of his grip was unexpected. "It doesn't matter."

"Like the devil it doesn't. You were ready to spend some time with me until I put my foot in my mouth."

She lifted her head with a snap. "You don't know that for certain."

"I had not thought you a liar." The game had become real, the emotions stinging with too much force to allow for discretion.

Cinnamon jerked her hand away, angered more deeply than she had been in a long time. "I think we've both said enough, especially here."

She headed for the hall, expecting him to stop her. When she paused, looking around for a phone, he was beside her.

"A coward, too."

"Add mistress to the lot and you'll have a tight summation of my character."

"Neither of you deny it, and you both must know what's being said." He saw the phone almost at the same moment she did. He pulled her bag from her fingers when she started toward it.

Cinnamon swung around. "Give that back."

Ben put it in his jacket pocket. "At your door."

"In your dreams."

"In both our realities because you won't make a scene here and we both know it. Your temper may be hot enough to explode but you won't let it." He reached for the door, opening it for her. "My car is the black Mercedes sports car at the end of the drive."

"I don't like you." She went out, as close to fury as she had ever been in her life. Getting outmaneuvered was a new experience and she didn't like the feeling at all. She was not a good loser.

"That makes us even. I don't like you, either."

Cinnamon stopped abruptly, her anger diluted by confusion and genuine curiosity. "Then why this?"

She jumped a little when his hands settled on her shoulders.

"Because I admire you. And despite what I'm not sure is the truth about your relationship with the senator, I respect you. Not *like*. Never such a tepid word." He gave her honesty because he could do no less. Her eyes demanded nothing less.

"I am not sleeping with him. I never have." The words were out before she could stop them, an explanation she had offered no one else.

Ben exhaled slowly, feeling relieved—along with something more—at the confession. She had cared enough to set the record straight. Another step. "Thank you." He pulled her close and kissed her lightly. He wanted more but he settled for less—for now.

Cinnamon let him hold her but didn't respond. Her emotions were out of control and she wasn't sure how she had lost her grip. This man was dangerous in a way she didn't understand. He looked so harmless, gentle, kind and easy to be with. With a few words he had tripped her temper, gotten under her guard and beaten her at the games she played and usually won. A coup.

When Cinnamon didn't say anything, Ben tucked her arm in his and urged her the rest of the way down the drive to the car. "Could I talk you into a nightcap somewhere along the way?"

Cinnamon settled in the passenger seat, waiting until Ben got into the car to answer. "I'm tired, really." Her fingers pressed lightly to her temples, massaging to relieve the dull headache.

"And from the looks of you, your head is pounding. Too much noise and too many late hours. Forget your job for a while and rest. Pretend I'm just a chauffeur.''

She smiled slightly, finding it surprisingly easy to follow his suggestion. Angling her head, she watched his smooth handling of the car. "I've changed my mind. I think I like you after all."

Mentally, Ben grimaced at the decision. There were many emotions that he wanted to aspire to with this woman, but *like* was not one of them. "Close your eyes and shut that pretty mouth before I forget my good intentions."

Cinnamon smiled at the mildly irritated command. Her resistance was low and yet she had never felt more safe. The silence with Ben beside her was the closest she had come to peace. Her lashes drifted down on the thought, and she slept.

Ben heard her breathing deepen. He wondered if she would realize how much trust she had displayed in him by going to sleep. For the purposes of his assignment, he should have been delighted. Having her trust would make uncovering her secrets a piece of cake. He glanced at her and came to a decision. He hadn't known the idea was in the back of his mind. A moment later he guided the car onto a side street—a street leading away from the direction of her apartment.

Ben pulled into the underground security garage of his own apartment. She didn't waken when he turned off the car's motor. He sat looking at her for a second, knowing he was taking a chance on blowing the whole case, but knowing, too, that he was going to accept the risk. Moving as quietly as possible he eased from the car and closed his door. So far so good. Then hers was opened and he lifted her carefully into his arms. She stiffened, half waking. He froze, holding her, watching her slowly relax again. The warmth he felt as she settled her head on his shoulder stunned him. Her breath teased his throat and her scent tantalized his senses as he carried her into the elevator. He reached his apartment without meeting anyone.

The lights were on in the living room, providing enough illumination for him to move down the hall to his bedroom. He could have used the guest room but he wanted her in his bed even if he was going to deny himself the pleasure of sharing it with her.

Cinnamon surfaced at the touch of coolness where there had been warmth. It took a second for her to identify the feel of the bed beneath her. "Ben," she murmured sleepily as she felt his arms withdraw. She was so tired. Her head hurt. The single glass of champagne she had consumed on a half-empty stomach, combined with the pain was making her too drowsy to move. "I don't want to sleep in this dress."

"I didn't think so. Relax. I'll help you off with it."

"You shouldn't."

"Honey, you are exhausted and you don't know it." He sat down beside her and lifted her into a sitting position, her head once again on his shoulder. The feel of her curled against him fanned the desire alight that had become a constant companion since that damn videotape.

"No, I'm not," she argued halfheartedly. The air was cold against her bare back as the zipper slithered down. She shivered and moved closer to his warmth. "Don't like cold. Promised myself I would never be cold again. Head hurts."

"I know."

Apollo, the professional, catalogued the reference to cold, knowing it was important. Ben, the man, touched the bright fall of hair, stroking her temple as he shielded her body with his while he finished undressing her. He made his touch as impersonal on her body as possible, glad the darkness protected her from his eyes. He had taken enough from her by bringing her here without asking. Only scanty bikini panties and a lacy camisole were left as he tucked her under the covers.

"Feels so good," she whispered as his fingers eased the headache.

"Sleep well," he said huskily, kissing her lightly before getting to his feet. There was just so much temptation a man could take. And Cinnamon, warm, soft and willing was more than his willpower was capable of handling.

Four

Cinnamon struggled up from the depths of the best sleep she had had in weeks. Something was not as it should be. Without moving, she eased her eyes open, trying to see in the darkness of her bedroom. What few shadows of the furniture she could make out did not belong. Puzzled, she reached across the bed to turn on the lamp, only to be more confused when her fingers simply encountered more mattress swathed in silk. Silk. She sat up abruptly. She didn't own silk sheets. She had better things to spend her money on than extravagant bed linen. This wasn't her queen-size mattress, either. This thing was the size of half a football field.

"He wouldn't," she whispered in the darkness as a horrible thought struck. She remembered Ben telling her to relax in the car. She also had a vague memory that was growing more vivid by the second: of being carried and finally being undressed and tucked in.

All but bouncing out of bed on the thought of the last, Cinnamon found the bedside table and lamp. She switched it on, expecting to see her seducer sprawled somewhere close by. Her fury built when she thought of the advantage he had taken of her.

But she was alone. The door was closed. The room silent, empty of all but her. Glaring, angry and confused, she glanced around. The sight of her clothes draped neatly across the chair, her shoes side by side on the floor, her handbag on the table beside the chair wasn't reassuring.

"I should have known better than to trust that man," she muttered, grabbing the dress and pulling it on without regard for the delicate fabric.

Her one wish was to find the rat who had brought her here and give him a piece of her mind. Jamming her feet into her high-heeled shoes, she picked up her handbag, then realized her favorite bracelet was missing. It wasn't on the chair. A quick look showed it hadn't fallen on the floor.

"I'm not leaving here without it."

She turned, searching the room. The glitter on the bedside table drew her. She reached for the bracelet, then froze. A note, which she had been too angry to notice before, was propped against the phone. She couldn't believe Ben's audacity so she read the words aloud.

I have a feeling you won't sleep through the night. Right now you probably want my head on a block. Sorry, I'm sleeping, too, alone. I hate cold beds. You're gorgeous when you sleep. Here's the

number and money for the cab. Think how good
you'll feel over tipping the driver to get even. I
would have liked to have had breakfast with you,
but I guess that's no go.

Ben

P.S. You don't snore but you do make the sexi-
est little whimpers I've ever heard.

Cinnamon swore one long drawn-out oath. She
couldn't remember ever being so angry. She stomped
out of the room, the effect spoiled by the padding
provided by the deep brown carpet. She stopped first
at the door directly across from the master suite she
had used. The guest room. Empty. The hall was in
semidarkness. The living room had even less light. She
stood for a moment, getting her bearings. Why she
didn't just switch on the lights, she didn't know.
Maybe she wanted to sneak up on the stinker, jerk him
awake. Her eyes narrowed, suddenly detecting the
form on the couch near the windows. Moving closer,
she realized it was Ben.

An arm was thrown across his face as he lay on his
back. The sheet barely covered what was obviously
nude territory—well-built territory at that. Her fingers crushed the note she still carried as she watched
him sleep so peacefully. She reached out, her fingers
brushing his shoulder. The warmth of his skin felt like
a flame. Jerking her hand back, she hovered, too angry to walk away and yet too caught by the defense-
lessness of his position to take her revenge.

Indecision. A new experience. Confusion. Equally
new. Bewildered at her reactions, she backed away one
step, then another, until she could no longer see him.

Why hadn't he taken the guest-room bed or the one he so carefully tricked her into? She shouldn't have cared. She shouldn't have even thought of the question. He had taken advantage of her. That should have been all she remembered. Without realizing it, she returned to the bedroom, shutting the door behind her.

Cinnamon swore again on realizing where she was. Her hand crushed the note and hurled it toward the table. It knocked over a small statue. The sound was unnaturally loud in the silence. She froze, not sure whether she hoped the noise had awakened him or that he slept on. Finally, she knew he had not heard. She stared at the bed. She could leave. She *ought* to leave. But she was tired and her headache was back. The clock beside the phone said three. She didn't even know where in Washington she was. Why waste time traveling back to her apartment? If he had intended doing anything he would have done it by now.

Even as she took off her dress, Cinnamon knew she was rationalizing. The idea irritated her, but it didn't stop her from climbing back into *his* bed. Tomorrow she would get her revenge—some way, somehow. The promise made her smile. It wasn't a nice gesture, but he had outmaneuvered her more than once. Now it was her turn.

The next time Cinnamon awoke it was truly morning. The sun was pouring in the window. The faint clatter of pots and pans told her where Ben was. Her eyes narrowed as she realized her door stood open. But then so did the bathroom door, which she hadn't noticed the night before. She turned her head to look at the clock. The white sheet of paper on the phone drew her eyes. She wasn't even aware of sitting up as she reached for the message.

I hope you like eggs Benedict. They're my favor-
ite. Clean towels already out. Take your time. But
I am serving breakfast at nine. I hate cold eggs.
Do you?

Ben

P.S. You might have tried not to make those little whimpers, but it didn't work. They're still
sexy. It's a good thing I like cold showers. But not
cold eggs. Hurry up.

That last did it. Cinnamon jumped out of bed and
wrapped the sheet around her like a toga. She stormed
into the kitchen.

"I was awake, you know, when you came into the
living room last night. I could feel the mayhem in your
heart. What made you change your mind?" Ben asked
as she swirled in, her eyes alive with temper and a
readiness to get even. He wanted her off-balance and
confused. Only then would he be able to slip beneath
her guard.

The calm words stopped her. Cinnamon glared at
him as she swept the tousled hair out of her face. The
sheet slipped. She made a strategic dive for one corner, managing to save her modesty. Ben grinned,
making no secret of his appreciation of the fleeting
show of satiny flesh.

"You are an unmitigated rat, a trickster and a cheat.
I should have tossed you off that damn couch on your
ear but I am too much of a lady to resort to your infantile tactics. I can't believe you would pull something like this. I can't believe *any* man would pull
something like this! Did it give you a thrill to undress
a nearly comatose woman? Of all the rotten, under-

handed, sly, deceitful…'' She was so angry her tongue got twisted on the words, reducing her rage to ineffectual sputtering.

Ben listened to the outpouring, letting her work off her temper. He didn't listen to the individual words; rather he watched her face, saw what she would have hidden if he hadn't slipped under her guard. There was confusion and a trace of fear there. One he expected, the other surprised and worried him.

"First of all, I did not enjoy undressing you. It was pitch-dark in that room. I did not turn on any lights to get a cheap peek, nor did I cop a feel. That dress would have been crushed if you had slept in it and you wouldn't have been comfortable. The only time I touched you was when I kissed you. You were awake then. As for bringing you to my bed—you were asleep in the car. You hadn't given me your address. I had to make a choice.''

Cinnamon stared at him. His relaxed stance belied his watchful look. "You could have awakened me,'' she snapped.

"Why?''

"I do not sleep in strange beds.''

"My bed is not strange. I'll grant you it's a little on the large size, but then so am I. I like to be comfortable.''

"You know what I mean so stop playing dumb and laughing at me.''

"I am not laughing.''

"All right, smiling then.''

He kept on smiling. "Your sheet is slipping.''

She glanced down, startled at the comment. One breast was all but unveiled. One tiny fold of silk covered the nipple and that was it.

"Damn," she swore. If she let go with either of her hands, she would show as much if not more. Walking was out of the question because the sheet was tangled around her legs. Frustration warred with embarrassment. She jumped when she felt the touch of Ben's hands on her shoulders. Lifting her eyes, she found herself staring at a bare chest.

"What are you doing?" she demanded, incapable of thinking clearly.

"Getting you out of a sticky problem." He draped his shirt around her, holding the front closed. "Drop the sheet and put your arms in. I won't look."

Cinnamon stared into his eyes, unable to believe him. For a long moment she just looked, seeing nothing but her own reflection. Then, slowly, her grip eased. The sheet slithered to the floor. His gaze never wavered. He simply stood there, holding his shirt, helping her, protecting her. A knot that had its beginnings in a dark past unraveled. Her anger died. Confusion deepened. Curiosity reared its head.

"Why?" she whispered.

"You'll come to me. But not on your knees. No embarrassment, no humiliation. I wanted you here. You are. It's enough."

"I don't understand."

"I can see that."

"I don't know you."

"Easily remedied."

She shook her head. "You don't know my schedule. For that matter, I don't know what you do for a living."

"But I told you last night."

"I *owe* you for last night."

"A warning?" His eyes laughed at her although his expression remained solemn, even faintly enquiring.

"I think it is."

"Not good tactics." He used the shirt to pull her closer.

Cinnamon braced her hands on his chest. "Oh, I don't know. Anticipation of revenge can sometimes be more potent than the real thing." She was crazy to play games with him, to allow him to tease her out of her anger, to enjoy the sparring.

"Keep on, woman, and I'm going to let go of this shirt. Then more of you is going to be touching more of me than I think you want."

She should have retreated then. She even intended to. Her tongue had other ideas. "Care to repeat that?"

"I told you once, I'm no gentleman."

"You couldn't have fooled me."

"What makes you think I didn't?"

"Circles. Riddles."

"Keeps you off-balance. I can sneak up on you."

"Now you're doing the warning. Why?" Some instinct, once a tool for daily survival, flashed a warning. She missed the signal in the tension and the excitement of taking Ben on.

"The hunt is always more stimulating if the quarry knows the traps."

"You are likely to lose with a philosophy like that."

He bent his head. "Maybe. I'm going to kiss you. Are you going to bite me or do something equally unpleasant?"

"Try and see. Be brave."

"Will I get a medal for valor under fire?"

She shrugged gracefully. She wanted to taste his mouth, to touch him. "Do you deserve one?"

His lips closed over hers, teasing rather than taking. Cinnamon stood still letting the sensation wash over her. Her fingers flexed on his skin, nipping into the flesh. Ben groaned softly, the moan flowing from his mouth into hers. The erotic sound touched her, softening her stance. Her hands slipped to his neck, his to her hips. The shirt fell open. Neither noticed as he drew her against his chest.

Cinnamon inhaled sharply at the contact. Passion normally held in check flared to life. She pressed against him, needing a closer contact, wanting him more than she expected. Ben lifted his head, smiling although it cost him a lot of effort.

"I still hate cold eggs."

Cinnamon opened her eyes. The desire in his matched her own. "Why?"

"Timing, beautiful. All things in their right time."

"And this isn't right?"

"You know it isn't. I might be able to get you into bed. But will you be happy when it's over? Will I? I like being able to look at myself in the mirror when I shave." He moved slightly to one side so that the hair on his chest dragged across her nipples. He couldn't see them but he could feel them. There was something decidedly erotic about denying himself the pleasure of looking at her.

"You answer one question and create ten in its place. I don't understand you."

"Do you want to?"

Cinnamon took her time replying. It should have been an easy question. No man had ever really tempted her from her course. "I think I do," she admitted finally.

"Then spend the day with me. I'll drive you to your apartment so you can change. Then we can have lunch and laze around, to take a drive, shop, visit museums, whatever."

Finally, common sense reasserted itself, and she recalled that her free time was limited. "I can't."

"Why?"

"Work. I leave for New Hampshire on Monday. I have a bunch of chores to do at home before I go."

"Then let me help."

No one had ever offered to help her do anything. Cinnamon was stumped. It was becoming hard to hold out against this man.

Ben wondered briefly if she realized how eloquent her expressions were when she wasn't watching them. He had gained more than he expected with his tactics and yet he also discovered a strange sense of self-disgust. If things had been different, he could have been honest. "I'm a dab hand at oven cleaning."

Startled, Cinnamon laughed. "Mine isn't dirty. I don't eat at home often enough to make it worthwhile cooking. The frozen-food section of the market and the microwave are more my speed."

Ben frowned, not liking the image because his own was the same. He knew how lonely and empty that kind of life was. On the other hand, he also knew that people like him and, he suspected, like Cinnamon, preferred their own company either by natural inclination or because of the demands of their careers.

"The food is really quite good," she murmured, misunderstanding the frown.

"I know. I travel a lot, too. I'm no stranger to a microwave." He shifted, easing her away. It was time for a change of subject. She would learn soon enough what his role in her life was and he would face her temper again. "You have two choices. Eat wearing my shirt or go change. I'm cooking breakfast now."

Cinnamon started buttoning his shirt together as he turned toward the stove. "I haven't driven you to lust yet so I think my appetite will win out over modesty this time."

He glanced over his shoulder, his eyes tracing the long length of leg beneath the shirttails. "You do like playing with fire, honey. I salute your courage."

"Not courage, hunger." She ambled to the refrigerator. "What can I do to help?"

"Set the table. Help yourself to anything you find in the fridge that appeals."

Ben started cracking eggs into a bowl. "The plates are in the cabinet over your head. The glasses next to it."

"Don't I get any coffee before I begin earning my keep?" Cinnamon opened a door and looked inside. The sight of expensive bone china surprised her. "These are your good dishes."

"My only dishes," he corrected.

Taking two cups and saucers down, she poured them each some coffee.

"Black, one sugar."

Cinnamon put his on the counter beside him, then leaned next to him to watch. "You do that very well for someone who doesn't do much cooking."

He glanced up, smiling at the careful probing. It suited him for her to ask questions so he answered. "My mother believed every man should be able to do for himself if he couldn't sweet-talk a woman into doing for him. She had this idea that a man might be the head of a family, but that the woman was the neck who turns the head."

Cinnamon blinked then laughed softly, her amusement growing as the remark sank in. "And the bone china?" she asked when she got her breath.

"My fault. I like classy things. Always have. Fortunately I don't have to deny myself my little idiosyncrasies."

"That could sound like boasting."

He glanced at her, pleased at the way she was relaxing her guard. "What do you think?"

She studied him, watching his eyes. She had learned a person gave away a lot with his eyes. Only Ben didn't. His were clear, calm, even faintly inquiring but they betrayed nothing. "I don't know you well enough...."

He caught her on the lame excuse. "You didn't get to where you are without being able to size up people."

Cinnamon shifted restlessly. Feeling hemmed in, she moved away from him. "I thought we were going to eat."

Ben turned fully around, studying her. "Why don't you want to answer the question?"

She glared at him, irritated at the way he was pushing. "Why is it so important to you that I do?"

"A man likes to know where he stands."

"Are you crazy? You don't stand anywhere except in front of a stove. I don't know you."

"You don't want to know me, you mean."

She started to deny it then stopped. "All right. I don't want to know you."

"Pretending I'm nothing more than a nice man who hasn't stripped you and taken you right here isn't going to work. Wearing my shirt is supposed to be some kind of test. If I don't jump you, then you can ignore me. It won't work. I won't let you pretend you can ignore me. You're as aware of me as I am of you."

"I am *not*."

"Prove it."

"I'm not getting caught in that trap."

"It's no trap. I don't operate that way in my personal life." He came toward her with slow, even steps.

Cinnamon held her ground, while instinct warned her to flee. She might admit to herself that he was right although how he knew her so well was beyond comprehension. "I don't want this."

"What 'this' are you expecting?" He stopped before her. "I'm a full-bodied male, with all the appropriate urges. You are half naked in my kitchen. You don't even know where you are, and you haven't asked. You slept in my bed last night. I brought you here but you chose to stay. Now tell me why you didn't leave."

"I don't have to tell you anything."

She nearly jumped when his hands came up to frame her face. She could have struggled but she didn't. Half of her was alive with anticipation. None of the men in her life had prepared her for Ben. The cautious, deliberate side of Cinnamon, that made a goal and achieved it no matter what the obstacle, said to hide. She should withdraw from the conversation and the man. For the first time in her life she ignored the dominant part of her nature and allowed the woman to emerge, tentatively, slowly and uncertainly. But she did emerge.

"What do you want from me?"

He smiled, letting his emotion show now that she had taken the first step. "Do you really want me to tell you that?"

She evaded the question. "I don't like surprises. I always need to know where I'm going and how I'll get there."

He shook his head. "If you really believe that, then you aren't as perceptive as I would have given you credit for."

There was that certainty again. It said he knew more about her than was possible after so short an acquaintance. Her gaze sharpened. This time she heeded the instinct that demanded an explanation. "I want to know who you are and what you're doing in my life." She pushed his hands away from her face.

"You won't like it." Ben always relied on his senses. Time and experience had taught him that procedure, plans and schedules were too limiting for the variety of human reaction.

Cinnamon still held his hands but she didn't notice. His tone had all her attention. The sexy drawl that had been a subtle threat was gone. This voice was all business, cool, empty. The change was startling and unnerving.

"Meaning?"

"Starting Monday, we'll be working together." Other than the tightening of her grip, he could see no response in her face. Again he acknowledged her expertise, her courage and her skill.

"How? We already have a security team for Don."

"And I have just been added to it."

"By whose orders?"

"You know."

"Does Don know?"

"He will be informed tomorrow by the chief of his security team."

"Yet you only fully told me the truth today. Why?"

"I don't like lies."

"Neither do I. Nor do I like being maneuvered. You were deliberately vague when I asked you who you were. You said you were with security, but you never said *whose* security."

"I wanted to see how close you and the senator are. When I was brought in, I was briefed. No one knew for sure. I needed to be, to do my job."

She dropped his hands then, angered, hurt and upset with herself because it did matter to her why and how he had come into her life. "I want to go home." She turned and headed for the door.

"I won't take you."

"Then I'll call a cab."

"Dressed in my shirt?"

The laugh in his voice and his words got her attention. She swung around. "Explain."

"I knew you'd be furious when I left that second note. Too furious to look for your clothes, not that you would have found them. I hid them," he said without a trace of an apology. "Check and mate, I believe."

"Don't count on it. I'll walk home in this if I have to." Right then she would have been capable of anything to escape. "That damn briefing of yours was entirely too comprehensive," she added for good measure.

"No, it wasn't." He closed the distance between them. "If it had been, I wouldn't have needed to trick you to discover if you were sleeping alone."

"You haven't really discovered anything." The hated rumor suddenly became wonderful camouflage.

Anger licked at the edges of his self-control as she caught his most vulnerable spot. He didn't want her to be Metcalf's mistress. The woman Jonathon believed her to be could be capable of sleeping with a man under the nose of his wife. But Ben couldn't buy the idea. Cinnamon was capable of a lot of things, but not that.

"You pick good weapons."

"I had a good teacher."

"The one who taught you to hate the cold?" He knew the moment he said the words that he had gone too far.

Cinnamon froze, her eyes narrowing to green chips of ice in a face so tight he hurt to see it. "Who told you that?"

He wanted to touch her; to take back the comment. He didn't dare. She was a breath away from running, hard and fast. He would catch her, but that fact would never be forgotten by either of them.

"You did. Last night. When I tucked you in."

His voice was soft, slow, gentle. Crazy though it was, she wanted to respond to the warmth, to the compassion she saw in his eyes. She wanted to call him a liar, but she couldn't. The truth was written in his expression.

"It didn't mean anything."

"I think it did. Won't you tell me?"

She laughed harshly. "I'm not crazy."

"No, you're hurting. Let me help."

"I don't need help." She backed away a step. "I don't know what you think you know, but I don't

need help. My life is going just the way I want it to."
Another step took her farther away from temptation.

Ben let her go. A few incautious words had lost all
the ground he had gained. "I'll take you home. You
can use the shower while I get your clothes." He
brushed past her, being careful not to crowd her. He
had done enough damage for one day. They needed
time apart. His to think and hers, he hoped, to forget
although he knew it was a vain hope at best.

Five

Cinnamon leaned against the door, staring at her living room without really seeing it. Her breath came quickly, as though she had just finished a long race. Her hands were flat against the door, her body tense. Ben was gone by now. His jaw had been tight, his voice silent, his eyes stormy with temper. They hadn't spoken as he had driven her home, back to the address he had said he didn't know. He hadn't asked her where she lived, and she had been so angry she hadn't noticed that he'd lied to her until they pulled up in front of her building. She had looked at him then, something she had avoided doing since getting into his car. She hadn't said a word; neither had he. Finally, when she couldn't bear the silence any longer, she had gotten out of the car. He had spoken. She had answered. A challenge. A parry. The game was again enjoined.

"I'll see you on Monday."

"I'll see you in hell."

He laughed grimly. "On Monday."

She had walked away, straining for the sound of his Mercedes leaving. But relief hadn't come. She had been able to feel his eyes boring into her back. She hadn't been conscious of hurrying until she had seen the look the security guard at the desk had given her.

Here she was: home. She should have felt safe, relieved, back on track or at least getting there. Instead, she was more confused, more angry, more torn by emotion than she had been before. His scent was on her skin. Suddenly she couldn't bear the fragrance. Pulling her clothes off as she went, she headed for the bathroom and stepped into the shower. A vigorous wash with her favorite soap helped the reality but not the memory. He had touched her.

She couldn't forget even for a moment that she had leaned on him. She leaned on no one. There was danger in dependence. Pain. Humiliation. Weakness was a victim's curse. She had learned strength from a victim's desperation. She didn't know how, but Ben knew those lessons, too. For the first time in her life as Cinnamon Cartier, she was afraid. Ben could—no, in fact he already had—hurt her. He understood things about her that no one else did. He was a danger from whom she would steer clear at all costs.

Cinnamon glanced at the phone. Calling Don and telling him what Ben had told her might get Ben in trouble with his superiors. Maybe, if she added the bit about last night, he'd be reprimanded or thrown off this assignment. He had given her the perfect weapon with the breach in protocol. Her hand hovered above the receiver. One call. A few words.

Linda answered. Cinnamon exchanged greetings before asking for Don.

"What's up Cinnamon? Problems?"

Both knew she wouldn't have bothered him if it hadn't been important.

"I heard something last night I thought you should know," she began slowly. "Have you talked to the security head this morning?" Now that she had started she found herself almost hoping that Don already knew. Then her guns would be spiked before she fired a shot.

"No. Why?"

"We'll be having a new man with us, apparently a kind of advance guard in New Hampshire. They intend to tell you tomorrow." Saying the words quickly didn't help. She still felt guilty, as though *she* were the wrongdoer and not Ben. Shifting restlessly, she fought the need to slam down the receiver. She had come this far. She would finish.

"So? I don't see the problem. It would have been better had they told me first but, selfishly, I'm glad they bothered you with the details instead. Linda and I have so little time together, as it is."

Cinnamon opened her lips to tell Don just how she found out and realized she couldn't go through with it. Don's low-key reaction was just the drenching with cold water she needed. Her temper fizzled and died to be replaced by weariness.

"Are you still there, Cinnamon?"

No, she wanted to say, but didn't. "I'm here."

"I'll mention the breach in procedure but I doubt that anyone will do anything. Besides, for all we know, the powers that be probably thought that telling you

was as good as speaking to me, especially since I'm
supposed to be relaxing."

"You're right. I overreacted."

"A little, maybe. But you're entitled. You're even
more tired than we are, and you aren't going to be able
to slack off now."

"I don't mind."

"I know. And I appreciate the load you've taken off
my shoulders more than I can say. Who knows?
Maybe this new man can help you a little. Let him
make himself useful."

The irony of his words almost made her laugh as she
hung up the phone. The last thing Ben was in her life
was useful. She lay down on her bed and stared at the
ceiling. She could feel the tumult of emotions inside;
knew that unless she could get a grip on herself, Ben
would make mincemeat of her defenses. She had to be
calm, cool and professional the next time they met.
Ben was a fact of her life for as long as security was
necessary or until he was reassigned. She had to find
a way to ignore him.

Ben stared at Jonathon, idly wondering if the man
would pop a blood vessel. He had never seen him so
angry.

"I thought you had more finesse. You just jeopar-
dized your own effectiveness. You're no rookie. You
must have had a reason."

"I did. Besides, what are you so upset about? We
learned a lot more with my so-called lapse than you're
giving credit for. For one thing, Metcalf didn't come
down on us breathing fire. He simply mentioned that
he preferred knowing our plans himself before they
were discussed with any member of his staff. Cinna-

mon Cartier included. His words not mine. I would think you would be pleased. Ms. Cartier doesn't appear to have as much influence over the senator as you thought.''

Jonathon glared at Ben over the tips of his steepled fingers. ''Or she is an extremely clever woman. I still don't understand why you took her to your house.''

''And I don't intend to tell you, either. Be satisfied I didn't try to lose the tail you had on her last night.''

''She is a beautiful woman.''

Ben knew it was time to leave. ''She is.''

''This is your last assignment.''

He smiled at the conclusion he knew Jonathon wouldn't say aloud. ''True again.'' He headed for the door.

''I don't like being nervous. It's not good for my ulcer.''

''Take an antacid.''

''I'd rather have your assurance.''

Ben paused to glance over his shoulder. ''I go my own way. That's how I've always worked. You know that. Tell me you want a report on every move and I walk. You know that, too. So don't push.''

Jonathon's glare deepened. ''I am your superior.''

''And I am insubordinate.''

He sighed, knowing when he was beaten. ''I don't know how a renegade like you survived in this business,'' he murmured, honestly puzzled. ''They should have thrown you out long ago.''

''I get results and I know where the skeletons are buried. Nasty combinations in anyone.''

* * *

"Nice try, Cinnamon." Ben leaned back in his chair, taking the precaution of holding the phone away from his ear.

"Who is this?" Cinnamon knew but she wasn't about to admit that Ben's deep, slow voice was that memorable.

He laughed at her blank tone. "At least you didn't hang up on me. I expected you to attempt breaking my eardrum."

"Don't bet I still won't," she warned, abandoning her childish pose. It had been a stupid move, at best.

"You didn't tell him I tricked you into sleeping in my bed."

"I would have, if I had been able to figure out how without making myself look even more naive and trusting than I ended up being. Not good images in my world."

Ben could hear the disgust as well as the truth in her admission. One he could tolerate, the other had to be put to rest.

"There is nothing wrong with trust or innocence."

"Says the wise man to the fool who knows better."

Cinnamon's bitterness hurt more than it should have. He had meant to reach her—not to hurt her. "I was the one in the wrong."

"An apology?" She laughed a little, feeling angry, sad and smarting from the blow to her pride. Until Ben had come into her life she had been sure she had protected herself completely. He had shown her just how flimsy her defenses were.

Frustrated at his inability to see her face, to touch her, to hold her in his arms, Ben half suggested, half ordered, "Let me come over."

"No way."

"An hour. I'll leave to the second. You can time me."

"Forget it." She pulled the receiver from her ear before she could give in to temptation.

"Don't hang up."

"Damn you for knowing what I'm going to do," she said just before she slammed down the phone.

Ben knew too much. Feeling exposed, needing to hide, Cinnamon paced the apartment. If she went out she ran the risk of bumping into Ben. If she stayed he couldn't reach her. He'd never get past security. She glanced out the window without seeing the spire of the Washington Memorial on the Washington skyline. She was tense and on edge. When the doorbell rang she jumped. She didn't need to answer it to know Ben had run her to the ends of the earth.

The bell rang again. She knew he wouldn't leave without seeing her, so she crossed the room in swift strides. It was better to get the confrontation over with.

"May I come in?" He watched her, making no move to force his way in. It was enough she answered.

"I'm surprised you asked."

He grimaced, acknowledging the thrust. "I deserved that, I suppose. We could go to neutral ground. I'd wait out here for you until you get ready, if you prefer."

"What I prefer is not to see you again."

"I know."

"No smart comeback?"

He raised his hands, palms up. "You can't fight with the truth."

"You wouldn't know the truth if it bit you on the nose." She wanted him to fight back. She needed the outlet for her seething temper.

"It's easy to lose sight of what's real and right."

She glared at him, frustrated at the soft, gentle answers. "Damn you. Push back. It's like punching out a marshmallow."

He shook his head. He smiled slightly, and his expression held more sadness than Cinnamon wanted to see. Her anger and feelings of ill-usage sputtered then caught again. She had been taken in by his acting once before.

"You won't get around me acting the penitent. Did they send you here to mend your fences?"

"Who's they?"

"You know who. And don't change the subject."

He leaned against the door, thereby bringing himself closer to her. He would go more slowly. Now, because he could afford to take his time. Jonathon was wrong. Now, all he had to do was prove it to everyone's satisfaction.

"I'm not acting."

Cinnamon could feel a change in the atmosphere, a subtle relaxation that hadn't been there before. It couldn't be coming from her, so it had to be from Ben.

"I don't trust you," she stated baldly.

"No reason why you should."

"Stop doing that."

"What?"

"Agreeing with me." Frustration deepened the edge in her voice.

Ben eased away from the jamb and reached out slowly. Her eyes widened at the move but she stood her ground. His fingers settled on her shoulders. "I pulled a trick on you. You tried to even the score by reporting my small breach in confidence. I got my hand slapped by my boss who's a by-the-book man. To my mind we're even. I don't hold grudges. Do you?''

"I'm surprised your briefing didn't cover that little quirk in my nature." She didn't want to believe him. Reflex made her strike back.

"That was a low blow."

Her conscience stirred. She tried to pull away from his gentle hold. His grip tightened without hurting. "It was," she admitted without intending to give an inch. His smile touched her more deeply than the feel of his hands on her bare shoulders. She stared at him, wanting to start over. "I shouldn't trust you."

"I'm not asking you to. Protect yourself. It won't matter. Eventually you'll see I'm no threat. I don't mind waiting."

"It will make working together easier."

Ben laughed then, relief stronger than he wanted to know coursing through him. "Rationalization?"

"Certainly not." She smiled as she spoke. He still touched her. She liked the feel of his hands on her shoulders, the humor in his expression, the peace he brought with him. Sighing, she realized she had very little quiet in her life, had never really wanted any before.

"Now, may I come in?" Ben wanted to ask what thought had slipped into her mind and stolen the lovely smile from her face. For one moment he had seen a woman without a care—a woman willing to laugh, to enjoy life instead of working nonstop for some goal known only to her.

Cinnamon glanced over her shoulder, hesitating.

"What's wrong?" He frowned, noting the resistance in the tense set of her shoulders.

"I don't really want to stay indoors," she murmured. "I was going out when the doorbell rang."

Ben kept his disappointment under wraps. "Then I should let you get on with your plans." He released her slowly and started to turn away. Her hand on his arm stopped him.

"No, wait. Would you like to come?" The invitation surprised her.

"Are you sure?" He watched her closely.

She nodded.

"Where?"

"I hadn't decided. I just need to get out. I'm not very good at staying home." She felt foolish at the admission.

Ben's face gentled at the faint flicker of embarrassment in her eyes. He doubted she had ever admitted her need of activity to anyone. "High-powered jobs tend to be addictive." He urged her into the apartment and shut the door behind him. "I assume you want to change."

Cinnamon glanced down at herself, having forgotten she wore a pink track suit. "That's kind of hard, since I don't even know where I want to go."

"I have an idea but I'm not sure you'll like it."

She studied him, seeing mischief in his eyes. "Why don't you tell me and I'll let you know," she invited, resisting the urge to grin like a kid.

"Can you fly a kite?"

"A kite? Me? You can't be serious."

Ben managed to look wounded. "I assure you I am. I have a friend who designs and makes the things. He's positive one of these days he'll come up with a really fabulous creation. He's always looking for responsible test fliers, and let me tell you, that isn't as easy as it sounds. Some of those ideas of his will run your legs off before, if ever, you can get them to stay aloft. Just the kind of activity for a lady feeling surrounded by walls and needing to do something.''

''But I don't know how.'' She protested without thinking.

Ben stared at her. ''You never flew one as a kid?'' The closed look on her face said more than the shake of her head. ''Well, then, you must try this. No one should miss the excitement of getting a kite running before the wind, or watching a gaudy, long tail flash across the sky. Get changed, woman, while I call my friend and have him drag out two of his best flyers.''

Cinnamon rarely took orders. This time she didn't even think of protesting as she headed for her bedroom. She wanted to be with Ben. She liked the feeling he created; the pleasure, the innocence—and not-so-innocent—emotions he generated in her. She smiled wickedly. And it was good business to establish a rapport with co-workers. She ignored the fact that she hadn't felt the urge to establish any kind of relationship with the other security people assigned to Don. After all, a woman could be too honest, she reminded herself.

Ben watched Cinnamon go to the next room, unable to understand what he had stumbled into. Almost every kid he knew flew kites, or at least knew someone who did, even in this high-tech age. How could Cinnamon have missed so basic an experience? He frowned as he dialed his friend. He hadn't come here today with his assignment in mind. He had intended that the day be strictly between Cinnamon and him. Yet now she had dangled a thread attached to a question mark right under his nose. He would have to follow the lead she'd given him.

"Can't your friend supply the kites?" Cinnamon asked, on reentering the living room to find Ben frowning as he hung up the phone.

Ben looked at her, struck once again at how exotic, how different in manner and bearing she appeared from most people. Even in jeans, knee-high leather boots and bulky white sweater, she had a presence that commanded attention. Although she stood completely still, there was a sense of energy held barely in check. He could see how inactivity would grate on her nerves.

"I got them. One of his sons will drop a pair at this place I know. We can fly there without landing in a nest of power lines or tangling with a bunch of Saturday merrymakers."

"In D.C.? You're a magician if you can pull this off."

He took the coat she pulled out of the closet and held it for her. The surprise on her face made him laugh. "I know it isn't exactly fashionable, but it's a habit I kind of like. Besides, it was another quirk of my parents. Dad was a great believer in taking care of Mom. She was an even greater believer in proving to him that she could take care of herself. The thing was she loved Dad and, in the interests of peace, made compromises. Then she found out she liked the extra attention. Of course, Pop knew and teased her unmercifully about it. That's when she told him he was the head of the family but she was the neck that did the turning. Shut him up, let me tell you!" For a moment, he laughed at the memory. "If you really hate it, I'll stop."

Cinnamon tipped her head, realizing that here was another first. She, like his apparently strong-willed mother, liked the little old-fashioned courtesies that Ben so freely employed. Odd. She would have disliked them in anyone else, but she couldn't tell him that.

"It doesn't bother me." The half-truth was the best she could do. Tucking her keys into her pocket after she locked her door, she walked with him at the elevator.

"Are your parents still living?"

Cinnamon gave him a startled look. "What brought that on?"

He shrugged, watching her without seeming to. "Remembering mine. Besides, if I have a flaw, it's incurable nosiness."

"What a statement—if you have a flaw indeed."

Ben knew an evasion when he heard one. He would let her get away with this one. "You cut me to the quick. Are you going to tell me you're lily-white?"

The sharp look she gave him warned that he had once again tread on tender ground. Cinnamon was like a minefield. Every step he took seemed destined to cause another obstacle. That was guilt on her face, swiftly concealed, but guilt nonetheless. Could he be wrong and Jonathon right? The thought sickened him. He didn't want to believe it.

Cinnamon brought herself under control. Ben had made a perfectly innocent remark. She was more tired than she realized if she was going to jump at every chance comment. "You already know my biggest flaw.

I'm not good at sitting still. How much longer until we get to this place you told me about?''

"Depends on the traffic," Ben murmured, gesturing at the clogged road ahead.

The sun was shining, and although the temperature was in the low forties, the clear skies made it seem warmer. A lot of people were taking advantage of the lovely weekend weather. The parks were filled, the streets alive with cars and pedestrians. Spring was just around the corner and everyone wanted to enjoy the glimpse of its promise.

"Give me another flaw," Ben suggested after he negotiated a tricky intersection. "And I'll give you one of mine."

"A novel way of getting to know each other." A man interested in a woman usually asked about her background. She leaned back, prepared to indulge in the game if it kept him away from the real questions. This way she could control the situation. "I don't sleep much—about four hours a night."

"You beat me by an hour. Always thought people who went for eight to twelve were missing a third to a half of their lives."

"You, too?"

"Something else we have in common."

"I don't like flying."

His brows rose at the confession. "How do you stand this campaign then?"

"I grit my teeth and remind myself that I wanted this from the time I was fourteen years old."

"That long? What did your family say to your ambition. It's not exactly the regular course for a woman."

Cinnamon glanced out the window. They were finally leaving the city. "I never told them," she said flatly.

Ben glanced sharply at her averted profile. "Why not?" If he hadn't been so startled, he might have chosen a more subtle way to probe. Cinnamon didn't notice his harsh demand. In so many ways, her past was stronger than her present.

"I didn't have a family as you know it. From the time I was six I lived in a series of foster homes." Cinnamon jerked around when she realized she had spoken aloud. She always tried to avoid her background. There was less chance of discovery that way.

"Your parents died?"

"You could say that." For just a moment she spoke the truth instead of the fiction she lived.

Ben frowned slightly. Her wording was odd, as was her expression. Her dossier had called her an orphan. Her reply told otherwise. Cinnamon looked stunned, almost afraid. Fear wasn't an emotion he would have associated with her. The sight of the park spread out before him wasn't welcome. He needed answers but time to get them had run out.

"We're here," he announced. Her relief was nearly a tangible force. He wanted to pull her into his arms and hold her until that lost look left her eyes. He wanted to tell her that the past didn't matter to a person who had built a life of her own. But most of all he wanted to protect Cinnamon. He knew she could and did protect herself, but he wanted to take that burden from her. He wanted to free her from whatever chains that made her so restless, so unable to find peace.

Six

_____

"Woman, for an amateur, you fly a mean kite." Ben lay down on the ground beside Cinnamon.

"Are you sure those stakes will hold?" Cinnamon stared up at the the scarlet geometric shape that was hers. Ben's rainbow striped creation soared a few yards beyond. The long strings of both kites were tied to pegs in the ground.

"I promise your baby won't get away. I use those tie down stakes all the time." He caught her hand and pulled her down to lie beside him. He could feel very little of her body through the bulk of their clothing but he found it didn't matter. He just wanted her close.

"We should have brought a blanket," Cinnamon murmured, wondering why she wasn't fighting his hold or for the way he had positioned her head on his shoulder.

"You plan too much."

"Another flaw."

Ben turned his head and pressed a kiss to her temple. "Depends on what you're planning."

Cinnamon angled her chin so that she could look at him. "I've enjoyed today. Thank you."

"My pleasure, lovely lady. The restlessness gone?"

"Like it was never there."

She lifted her hand to his chest, giving in to the need to touch him. Physical contact wasn't always easy for her. She had spent so much of her life being just barely tolerated, that she had learned not to reach out to people for fear of being rejected. With Ben she had wanted to try. She still didn't trust him completely, but she was beginning to relax her guard around him— enough to allow him to link his fingers with hers, to lie beside him and want him to come closer.

Ben lay still, conscious of her hand on his jacket. This was the first time she had voluntarily touched him. The male in him was elated, the professional that needed more answers was pleased. "How about coming out to dinner with me tonight? I know this great little Italian place."

"I don't know."

"You enjoyed yourself today and so did I. Why not?"

"You'll think I'm naive, but I feel rushed." She laughed slightly, without humor. "I'm a planner. I don't fly through life like those kites, but I suspect that you do."

"I want to be with you."

"Because of the job?"

"Partly, but mostly because of you." Thankfully she had phrased the question so that he didn't have to lie.

She looked into his eyes. The desire she saw there didn't frighten her—the strength of will did. Both excited her, and in different ways. She sensed that Ben, in some strange respect, was stronger than she was. She sensed, too, what she saw was only the tip of the iceberg. If she had been playing by her old rules, she would have run long ago. But this was a new game. The plans of a lifetime were near fruition. Perhaps it was time to look for new fields to explore, new challenges to face, new odds to beat.

"All right."

He sighed deeply, this time his lips finding her mouth. His need to possess was compelling. He took what she gave and asked for more. Her moan of pleasure tightened the muscles in his body, heating the desire a notch higher. His hands moved under her coat, curling into the downy softness of her sweater and the lush flesh beneath.

Cinnamon pushed closer, needing his warmth. Her fingers slipped the buttons of his coat free so that she could burrow against his chest. He laughed softly, his breath stirring the hair. "I'm cold," she whispered—a lie and a truth mixed.

"So am I, in more ways than I'd better count right now." Ben savored the feel of her pressed against him before sanity reared its determined head: Cinnamon still had someone tailing her. The man was probably taking pictures right now. Ben didn't like the idea but it was a fact of life. So far, a kiss or two was nothing. But a few more of Cinnamon's enticing wiggles and those photos would need an X rating.

"Come on, honey. We'd better get those kites down and us home so we can change. Italian food is waiting." He set her away, unable to resist the urge to kiss the tip of her nose.

"That makes me feel about ten years old."

"You don't feel ten years old to me, I promise you," he returned with a thoroughly masculine grin. He got to his feet and pulled her up beside him.

She grinned, glad that he found her desirable. "Your mind is always on your basic urges," she accused, following him to where they had tethered the kites. She looked up. "I wish we didn't have to take them down."

Ben watched her, gazing at the kites. She was much softer than he had allowed for. The woman she had always seemed to be was nowhere in evidence now. This woman was vulnerable. She was not gentle, she was too strong a personality for that, but he had never particularly admired gentleness; too often it masked a cloying sweetness he found difficult to swallow. Better the mild sting of tartness, the exhilaration of a challenge.

"You've enjoyed yourself."

She turned her head, smiling. "You doubt it? I think half the city heard me shriek when I got that thing aloft."

"Maybe we should explore some more games you missed in your childhood," he suggested. He reached for the string of his kite as he spoke. He felt her freeze up a little, then sigh.

"You wouldn't have to look far. I did more working than playing." She, too, turned away to start reeling in her toy.

"Poor?" He kept his voice neutral and his eyes on the rainbow shape at the end of the line.

"Sometimes."

Had she meant to be vague? A quick glance suggested that she hadn't. She had told the truth.

"Does my past matter so much?" she asked.

He looked at her, choosing his words with care. "I want to get to know you. Is that so very odd?"

"No. But no one—" She stopped, unwilling to go on.

"No one what? Ever asked? Ever cared enough to ask?" The man more than the professional needed the answers to the questions.

"I don't like remembering. It wasn't a good time for me. I did things I'm not very pleased with." Cinnamon moved restlessly, wondering why she was telling him so much. Wondering, too, why she cared what he thought or felt.

"So?" The professional took over. "Every kid does things that aren't too great. That's what growing up is all about."

"Perhaps." She shrugged, wishing she hadn't opened up.

Ben was satisfied with what he had so far. Cinnamon had brought up more questions but at least she was talking. He kept the atmosphere light as they drove to her apartment. He left, promising to pick her up in three hours, which was just time enough to report to Jonathon.

Ben related the facts he had been able to glean as he sipped a light whiskey and water while he listened to the silence on the other end of the phone.

"That doesn't sound too promising."

"It's more than Briggs and Jeffries got. By the way, you can call off your tail now. I've got her." He didn't like the idea of the other operatives on the case talking among themselves about the budding relationship he was developing with Cinnamon. He wanted to protect her from the male gossip and speculation.

"That's not procedure."

"I don't care. I am not providing a peep show for yours or their amusement."

Jonathon sighed audibly. "You know we don't work that way."

"I know that we aren't *supposed* to work that way," he corrected, not prepared to budge on the point.

"I could pull you."

"Go ahead. See how far you get with her."

Ben counted on his past service, his reputation, and the fact that he knew the right people, to lend credibility to the threat he wouldn't have made to anyone else. He had a measure of how much Cinnamon influenced him by his willingness to force Jonathon into a corner. His reputation could be on the line if he was wrong.

"What about when you aren't with her?"

It was a compromise. "One man. Briggs."

"You aren't letting her get to you, are you?"

Ben had been expecting the question before now. He had seen the speculation in Jonathon's eyes. "Does it matter as long as I do my job?" he asked bitterly, before hanging up. He finished his drink in one gulp and wished it were straight liquor. He swore once, long and hard, before getting up to shower and change.

"Have I told you how beautiful you are tonight?"

Cinnamon gazed into Ben's eyes, forgetting for a moment the homey atmosphere of the small restaurant around them. The candlelight was kind to his face, although he didn't really need that gift.

"No." She smiled slightly. "Not in words, anyway."

He grinned. "Was I leering when you opened the door?"

"A little."

She shrugged, trying not to betray just how much she had enjoyed his blatant approval of the slim-fitting gold dress she had chosen. The fabric was nearly the same shade as her skin. While not tight, it clung in all the right places. It wasn't a gown she chose to wear lightly. Why she had picked it for this evening was still in doubt. She had enjoyed herself so much today just being with him. Desire had lurked just below the surface but the fun of flying the kites and the way they had played had been the part she remembered. All that made her behavior now all the more incomprehensible. Tonight she wanted to see the light of desire burn in his eyes. And it was. It was in the way he watched her. It filled his husky voice.

"Did you mind?"

She laughed softly. He had her cornered. "Damned if I say no and damned if I don't. I think you are a sneaky man." She frowned at the shadow of displeasure that crossed his face. "Did I say something wrong?"

Ben made himself smile. "No. I was just trying to envision myself as sneaky." He glanced around the restaurant, cursing the flicker of pain that had made him betray himself. A rank rookie would have been in better control. "What do you think of the place?"

Cinnamon studied him, uneasy at the way he seemed to be avoiding her eyes. "It's delightful," she said slowly, looking for a clue in his reaction. "Ben, is there something going on with Don you aren't telling me?'' she asked suddenly.

This time he didn't betray his surprise. He turned casually. ''Not that I know of. Why?'' The wariness was back in her eyes. He damned his stupidity again.

''You looked...'' She spread her hands, unable to come up with an adequate explanation.

''Maybe I was trying to figure out how to maneuver you into my bed again.'' He had to stop her probing and that meant giving her another target.

Cinnamon stared at him, caught short by the blatant invitation in his look and words. Her uneasiness doubled. The pass didn't match the man she thought she was beginning to know. Either her judgment was off, or... She didn't want to think about the possibilities.

''I think you're lying.'' She could have cursed when the waiter arrived with their order. She sat back almost positive Ben was relieved at the interruption. Her eyes narrowed. Was Don in some kind of trouble? Had there been some threats to him or the family?

''As you wish.'' Ben shrugged as though it didn't matter. His herring hadn't worked. She was looking even more suspicious.

''What kind of threat is it?''

''I don't know what you're talking about.''

''You aren't a replacement. You're an addition. Why else would Don need beefed-up security unless some looney wants to make mayhem?''

''Just suppose for the sake of argument you're right?'' He watched her pale. ''What do you expect me to tell you? You know the rules, or should.''

''I expect you to be honest.''

''Are any of us ever completely honest?''

There were a hundred ways a person could hurt Don—through Linda, the twins, or even through her, although the last was of lesser importance than the others.

"I thought we were."

"Is that trust I hear, oh doubtful woman?"

Cinnamon drew back, not expecting the sarcasm nor the hurt that followed. She laid down her napkin, needing to put some distance between them.

"Running, Cinnamon?"

"Yes." She half rose in her seat, stopped only by the hand that snaked out to snag hers. His fingers were like handcuffs around her wrist. She wanted to fight the hold. Only the realization that anyone could be watching made her subdue the reaction and settle for a lethal glare.

"I did not have you pegged for a coward."

"I'm a survivor. There is a big difference."

Ben searched her face. This was the woman he had seen on the videotape, the one who manipulated a man and an entire family from across the room, the female that had a number of people shaking in their boots over her influence. Yet he saw more this time. He saw the worry beneath the anger, the pain under the temper. His hold gentled.

"Sit down."

"No."

"I can make you. I don't want to, but I can."

She inclined her head. "The body isn't the same as the mind. I think you're smart enough to know that. Besides, aren't you the man who said he didn't want me on my knees."

"You know where to hit."

"Street knowledge. Anyone learns when they have to."

He tugged gently. "And you did?"

Cinnamon sat down. "I had no choice. I had no home after I was fourteen. That's a risky age for a girl." She pulled her hand from his grasp, immediately missing the warmth when she expected to be glad for her freedom. She stared at her wrist, confused at the reaction.

"You won't let anything happen to Don, will you?" she asked without looking up. "Linda and the twins would be devastated."

Ben inhaled sharply at the anxiety in her voice. She really cared for the man. "Does it matter that much?"

She raised her eyes to his. "Yes. He gave me a chance when no one else would. Even now, there are more experienced men out there eager to get their hands on him and his campaign. He still believes in me. Yes, it matters."

"You love him?"

Startled, shocked that he could think such a thing, Cinnamon could only stare. "No."

"You're sure?"

"Does it matter?"

"Yes."

"You're crazy."

"Probably. I want you. I haven't made any secret of that fact. I think you could want me if you would let yourself, in spite of the fact that you don't completely trust me. But something besides your natural caution is holding you back."

"You know the kind of life I lead."

Ben picked up his fork and began to eat. "I do. But I'll be leading the same kind of life—at least for the time being. What's wrong with us traveling the same road together?''

Cinnamon took a bite of her lasagna, too involved with what he was saying to notice she was eating. "I don't do things like that."

"Like you don't fly kites?"

"Don't be facetious."

"Talk to me."

"What do you want me to say? That I want you, too?"

"It would be a start." He glanced up to pin her with his stare. "You like honesty, remember?"

Cinnamon shook her head, fighting for a smile. Ben had a way of defusing her temper she could neither understand nor, it seemed, fight. "I don't know how you do it. A moment ago I was ready to hit you—or worse. Now you've got me involved in a crazy discussion. I can't take you seriously over spaghetti and lasagna. The setting lacks something, but your ability to march through my emotions doesn't. You're really beginning to worry me."

"You can handle me if you quit trying to run."

"Dutch comfort?"

"Truth." He wouldn't let her go. There was an urgency he didn't understand driving him to forge a bond of passion, if nothing else, with Cinnamon.

"All right you want truth. Yes, I want you, but I'm not going to do anything about it."

He laughed slightly. "That dress says you're lying through your beautiful teeth."

Those beautiful teeth snapped together with an audible click. Ben laughed again. Lord, the woman was glorious. She had more twists than a crooked road and he loved every one of them. The man who held her heart would have to be on his toes every minute of the day and night. She would lead him around by the nose if he let her and make him love every minute of the enslavement.

"I said it before, but it bears repeating. You are a rat, Ben Forsythe." She fought the grin tugging at her lips and lost.

Ben lifted his glass in a toast. Cinnamon raised hers to touch his. "I may be a rat, but you want me."

"And I am not going to take you."

"We'll see." He picked up his fork again. "Eat your dinner. You're going to need all your strength."

"I'll eat, because suddenly I'm hungry not because I think I'll need any extra strength."

"I've heard passion hits some women that way."

Cinnamon didn't need her *t*'s crossed. "You'll never be sure."

"Do you gamble?"

She blinked. "No."

"Too bad. We could have bet on the outcome."

She laughed then. It was impossible not too. For the rest of the evening she vacillated between temper and good humor. Ben played her and she played him. Neither racked up an impressive score but then neither surrendered. By the time he dropped her at her door with nothing more than a chaste kiss on the forehead, Cinnamon wasn't sure whether he was a devil or a saint. She did know one thing. She had a blouse that would raise a corpse's blood pressure that she could wear when they went kiting tomorrow. She'd show him a thing or two about wanting and having.

Ben lay in his bed, staring at the ceiling. Cinnamon had taught him things tonight that he hadn't known mattered. She had taught him the value of a woman's quick mind. She had made him think, plan. Her thrusts were sharp, potentially lethal. She enjoyed the challenge of everything he tossed her way and didn't mind in the least when he bested her. She simply redoubled her own efforts to return the favor. She was gracious, whether in winning or losing.

And Cinnamon the woman was a beautiful creature who seemed unaware of her attraction to the opposite sex. Despite wearing a dress that had to have come straight out of a diabolical mind, she had used no tricks to tease. Her sensuality was as natural as the color of her hair, and all the more potent because it invaded every breath she drew, every gesture she made, every word she spoke.

His body loved the feel, sound and taste of her. Even now he still hurt in parts of his anatomy that he would have preferred to forget. Cinnamon's memory had survived two cold showers and a shot of bourbon. He had a feeling it would also survive a long, restless night.

Seven

"Where shall we go for dinner tonight?" Ben asked as he and Cinnamon got into the car.

The kites were stowed in the back seat. The leisurely morning and the afternoon picnic had been relaxed and filled with laughter. Cinnamon had again thrown herself into the exercise of getting her wind craft aloft. Only this day she had a vaguely star-shaped affair of a ruinous green and baby pink that seemed to prefer land travel to air currents.

"I don't care where we eat as long as whatever I order doesn't fight back. I've about exhausted my patience for the day," she said ruefully, leaning back with the tired sigh. Her hair was probably sticking out in seven directions, any lipstick she had on was long gone and she knew for a fact she was sporting at least four separate grass-stain smears on the rear of her slacks.

"You never warned me that kite flying could be hazardous to my well-being." She used a bit of waning energy to open her eyes to glare at Ben when he laughed.

"I told you running down that hill wasn't a good idea. We had rain last night and it's cold. It's a wonder you didn't break your neck instead of bruise your dignity."

Cinnamon patted her abused anatomy gingerly. "It isn't my dignity that's smarting."

Ben couldn't resist Cinnamon's appeal. She was definitely worse for wear. The tip of her nose was sunburned. She looked as if she had come through a hedge backward, but—grass smudges and all—he had never seen her look lovelier. Leaning across the small space separating them, he kissed her gently, tasting rather than taking her lips. Her soft sigh was a sweet surrender he hadn't expected. He deepened the kiss as he drew her into his arms.

Cinnamon came to him, realizing she had been waiting for this all day. Every time Ben had touched her—even in the most innocuous ways—she had wanted to step into his arms, to feel his mouth on hers. Threading her fingers through his hair, she pulled him closer. She hardly noticed Ben lifting her into his lap. She did notice her sore derriere coming into contact with his taut thighs. She tried to muffle her groan.

Ben heard the small sound. He raised his head, smiling slightly at her grimace. "Sorry, honey. I forgot."

"I did, too," she admitted huskily as she shifted to a more comfortable spot.

Ben looped his arms around her but didn't let her move back to her side of the seat. "Come home with

me. I can promise you a cushion in front of the fire
and a good dinner.''

Cinnamon stared into his eyes knowing the time for
a decision had come. He had given her space to find
her answers. She didn't know him completely and yet
she wanted him. She didn't trust him completely and
yet she wished she could. It was less than she would
have liked, but more than she had ever had with any
man. Was she brave enough to take the risk?

"All right," she murmured slowly, looking for but
not finding even a hint of triumph in his expression.
All she saw was pleasure and relief. She smiled tentatively, feeling oddly uncertain.

Ben touched the faint furrow between her brows.
"Don't worry. I promise everything will be fine."

"Guarantees?" One eyebrow rose.

"You know better. Only a promise that I'll do my
best to keep. Neither of us believe in fairy tales. There
are more trolls than beauties in the world, and more
villains than princes. We take our chances on slaying
the dragons."

"You're almost as great a cynic as I am." She leaned
her head against his shoulder. "Do you ever wish you
could have your illusions back?"

Ben stroked the bright fall of her hair, smoothing
the wind driven curls against her head. "No. Sweetness and light are boring as Hades can be. I like the
contrasts. I wouldn't want a world of all black-and-
whites. I couldn't live up to the demands."

"But it's so simple. One would always know where
he was." She snuggled into his arms, liking the sooth-
ing stroke of his hands over her hair and down her
back. She felt safe, protected, yet not diminished by
her need to be held. Ben made her feel gentle but not

submissive, soft but not weak, and better than she knew herself to be.

"Perhaps. But there are so many things that won't fit in either category. Important things. Ultimately good things."

Cinnamon raised her head to search his eyes. Without realizing she meant to touch him, she lifted her fingers to his face and traced the lines that told the story of his passage through time and experience. Some of the marks were deeply etched, burned perhaps, by pain or sorrow. Other tracings were light, indicating shifts of mood only.

"What did you do before you were a security man?"

"A little bit of a lot of things."

"You always answer my questions vaguely."

"I don't like talking about my past any more than you do. Another thing we have in common." Ben lowered his head to take her lips. He didn't want to lie to her any more so he drove the thoughts from both their minds in the only way he knew. When he lifted his head, they were both breathing heavily.

"Let's go home."

Cinnamon silently slid off Ben's lap and strapped on her seat belt. Her lips were tender from his kiss. She ran her tongue over them, liking the feeling, liking knowing he was just as affected by her. She turned so that she could watch Ben as he drove.

"I wish you wouldn't do that," he said, glancing at her. "When you stare at me like that I get ideas that belong in a better time and certainly a more comfortable place."

"What kind of ideas?"

Ben laughed and caught her hand, trapping it against his thigh. "I wouldn't ask that if I were you."

She laughed, too. "All right. Tell me instead what we're having for dinner."

"Shrimp scampi."

"I'm drooling already."

"Do you want to go by your place to change?"

Cinnamon hesitated, then decided she wanted to know the truth. "You asked me about the bag I was carrying when you picked me up. It was a change of clothes," she admitted.

Ben glanced at her, his eyebrows raised. "Why didn't you say so then?"

"Would you believe I was nervous?" She looked away from his face, to stare out the window.

His fingers tightened over hers. "I'd believe it because I'm a victim, too. Damn disconcerting at my age, let me tell you."

Cinnamon swung around, surprised. "Really?"

"You matter to me, I told you that."

"But we wouldn't have met without your job."

"Or yours."

She nodded. "Maybe I ought to thank your boss for sending you to us."

"I don't think Jonathon would . . ."

"Jonathon? I thought the head man was . . ."

"He is." Ben would have liked his own tongue on a stick for the mistake he had made. "Jonathon is my immediate supervisor, that's all."

"Oh." She leaned back in the seat. "Tell him I said 'Thank you,'" she teased. "Just don't tell him why."

"Don't be cute."

"Temper, temper. I was only joking."

Ben pulled himself under control. The last thing he wanted was for Jonathon and Cinnamon to get together.

Cinnamon pulled her coat more tightly around her. "Can you turn up the heat? I'm freezing."

Ben automatically reached for the control. He should have remembered. For the past two days he had been keeping the thermostats higher for Cinnamon. "I can't get it much warmer. We're almost to my place, so hang in there."

Cinnamon grimaced at her quirk. "I keep hoping my blood will thicken up or something."

"How did you survive as a child in school? As I recall, the classrooms were unbearably hot in summer and hideously cold in winter."

"I wasn't in school that much."

Ben hesitated. As with all her confidences, he wasn't sure how far he could push. "Why? Sick?"

"No."

"Moving?"

Cinnamon shook her head. "I don't know why I talk to you. Do you know that there is no one in Washington that knows as much about me as you do? No, I didn't move, nor was I sick. I ran away—every chance, daily sometimes."

"Why? Was home that bad?"

Cinnamon felt the memories, fought them and lost. "Yes, more than I'll ever allow myself to talk about." She pulled her hand from his, unable to bear the contact. The sight of the underground garage of his apartment was both a relief and a curse.

Ben parked the car, then turned to face her. Cinnamon wasn't keeping to her supposed background. Every time he caught her unaware she seemed to be answering for another woman. More than ever, he was convinced that she not only hadn't always been Cinnamon Cartier but that she also couldn't be what Jonathon thought. "Have you ever told anyone about it?"

"No. And I won't."

"You should. It's hurting you."

Cinnamon edged away, opening the door to get out. The interior of the car was too close for comfort. Ben joined her, urging her toward the elevators. "Just leave it. It has nothing to do with us."

He pulled her into his arms as soon as the door shut. "It does. Let me help you."

"I don't need help."

"You're shivering right now."

"So? I'm cold."

"It's not cold in here."

He was right. It wasn't. "You're making me angry."

"Then lose your temper. Don't quiver like a beaten dog." If he hadn't begun to suspect at least part of the problem, he would have missed her faint reaction. For a woman as strong as she was, for one so independent, there had to be a reason she avoided contact. "Who was it?"

Cinnamon knew she had given herself away. For years she had sought and succeeded in erasing her past. Ben had ripped the veil of mystery to shreds. "No one."

"Your father?"

"Leave it." She wrapped her arms around her body as the tremors became full-grown shakes.

Ben took her weight against his chest. "Your mother?" The ripple of pain and fear filled the silence making a verbal answer unnecessary. He swore once before lifting her into his arms.

"Put me down. I can walk."

"Like the devil you can." He strode out of the elevator as soon as it stopped. "Get the key out of my pocket and open the door."

Cinnamon had never heard him speak in that tone before. For once, she took orders. Ben kicked the door shut and crossed the living room to the hall and then down it to the master suite at the end. He carried her to the bed and came down with her, pausing only long enough to yank the comforter that lay at the foot over them.

"You're nuts," Cinnamon said fighting the enveloping folds of satin.

The professional had ceased to exist in the garage. Only the man remained. "First we get you warm enough to stop shaking like a leaf in a hurricane and then you are going to tell me this deep, dark secret of yours so you can drag it out of the dark and let the scar heal. It's time. So don't even think you can stop me."

He glared down at her, too angry to worry about her feelings, too worried to consider his assignment, too caught in the trap of his own emotions to be kind. "Whether you know it or not it's going to be hard for me to listen to this."

"Then don't."

"Someone has to. I'm here and I'm not afraid of you."

"Damn you." She didn't want to know that she was relieved he was forcing the issue. She didn't feel safe enough to speak of the past. She didn't want to let him in this way. A lover, she could handle; a man to trust scared her witless.

"We both may be." He threw his leg over hers, stilling their restless movements. Caressing her cheeks, he looked into her eyes. "You've got more courage than most men. Stop running. I dare you."

"I'm no child to be tempted with those words," she snapped, taking refuge in temper. She knew as well as he that it was a delaying tactic. The warmth was seeping into the cold. The trembling was ceasing. The time for the truth was upon her.

"I can't."

"You will."

"You don't know what you ask." Her eyes burned. Damn! She wouldn't cry.

He touched the corners of her lashes. "Get it over with, love."

The tears trickled down her cheeks. "It was my mother. I was six when she disappeared out of my life. I was told she was dead. I never knew for certain. I landed in a series of foster homes, not the well-run ones they have now but the places where kids are an extra source of income. I'm not blaming the people who put me in the situation. They had no more choice than I. I was a tough child by then. Hard to handle. Withdrawn. I made trouble. By the time I was in high school I ran away more often than I stayed in one place. The foster parents couldn't put up with that kind of behavior. I was sent back to the main house and labeled incorrigible. I hate that word but I did my best to live up to it." She shuddered at the last and most hurtful memory. "Then nature entered the picture. I had been a scraggly preteen, but one morning I woke up and stared into the mirror. It was like looking at a stranger. The boys teased me, the girls hated me. What had been bad before, became a living nightmare. Finally, I couldn't take it any longer and I took off for good."

"But how did you live?"

"I lied about my age. Got a job in a bar, cocktail waitressing. Good money in that kind of work. Lots of long hours. I saved so I could go to school—real school. College. I wanted an education so badly. I wanted to be somebody. But most of all I wanted to be safe. I'll never be that vulnerable again. Never!" Cinnamon closed her eyes, feeling more tired than she ever had in her life. She was warm, drained and sleepy. She didn't understand her feelings, but she did acknowledge them.

Ben felt her sigh as she relaxed against him. He could tell by her limp position and the deadness of her voice that relating her story had exhausted her. The words had been simple enough—not horrifying at all, really. But their very starkness had emphasized the forces that had created the woman she had become.

For the first time Ben faced the fact that she very well could do what Jonathon believed she had done. Her motivation was certainly strong enough. She would have no reason to care about anyone or anything beyond her own needs. The system that should have protected her had shown itself woefully inadequate. The people she should have been able to trust to keep her safe and protected had let her down in the worst possible way. Everything she achieved or owned she had gained by her own methods. He knew enough about street kids to realize probably some of what she had done had shaved the meaning of the word *legal*. Cinnamon had survived but by her own rules.

Ben glanced down at her, realizing that she'd fallen asleep. He leaned back on the pillows, and pulled her more comfortably into his arms. For the first time in his memory he had a completely vindictive wish: that Cinnamon's mother would fry in a hell three times worse than that she had bequeathed her daughter. As for himself? He had the facts he needed but not the name of the woman she had been before she became Cinnamon Cartier. And where was the real Cinnamon? The background Jonathon had checked seemed real enough, although it was very incomplete.

Cinnamon stirred, feeling warm and secure, rested in a way that she seldom knew. Ben held her. She knew that, too. His body cradled hers, giving heat and a kind of caring she was coming to associate with him. Lifting her head, she tried to make out his face in the darkness. The features were indistinct, but it didn't matter.

"How long did I sleep?" she asked huskily.

"Two hours or a bit more. Why?" He hadn't been sure she wouldn't fight him when she awoke.

Cinnamon ignored the question to roll completely onto him. "Why are you so patient with me?" Need was building in her. She had already made her decision.

"I told you," he responded warily.

"Most men would have pounced."

"And you would have sent them running. You aren't a woman to force."

"My personality doesn't bother you?"

"I like it." It wasn't his imagination. She was reaching out to him in a way he hadn't expected. In a way he had been half prepared to have her push him away. And yet she seemed unaware that she hadn't given him the story of Cinnamon Cartier the way it would be in her dossier. Was it possible she didn't realize the slip? Or did she realize the slip and hope to deflect him with more than words? He wanted to trust her. If he could have seen the expression in her eyes, maybe he would have had his answer.

"I'm not an easy person."

"Is that a warning? I could say the same about myself. Would you run?" This was no game this time. She was serious. Whatever her reason for wanting him, it wasn't because she realized she had betrayed herself.

"No, I haven't. I won't."

He risked pulling her close, with her mouth inches from his own. "You're sure?"

"I never go forward until I am."

"Riddles. Even now you keep me guessing." No, she wasn't easy. She would lead him a long path. He wanted nothing less.

Cinnamon lowered her head, taking his lips as he had taken hers so many times before. She wanted to return the pleasure he had given her and reach higher with him than she had ever traveled with any man.

Ben let her come to him, understanding that she needed the initiative this first time. No, she would not kneel—ever. She would walk beside him, outrun him if he let her, but she would not submit to him or any other. Pride filled him because she had chosen to come to him. His tongue met hers in the most basic mating dances. Her body twisted over him, making a mockery of the outer clothes they still wore. Her hands flowed over him, releasing buttons as she sought to deepen the contact between them.

Ben moved then, slipping her coat from her shoulders, followed by her sweater and jeans. The room was warm but not enough to hide the chill of the small separation when he stripped his own jeans, dropping them carelessly on the floor.

"Cold, honey?" he whispered, as she held out her arms to embrace him. The covers were rumpled around her, the satin caressing her skin. "I'm glad you want me tonight. Touching you is more pleasure than I have ever known with another woman."

"I have never wanted another as I want you."

Neither of them pretended it was the first time, simply because both realized that none before mattered.

Ben kissed her deeply, eager now to touch the heaven and the hell he knew waited in her arms. His tongue sought hers, stroking and enticing her into the love play he wanted. Cinnamon met him halfway, twisting against him so that his body stroked hers with every breath he took. She wanted nothing between them.

His body was hard, his muscles tight with desire as she lingered over each curve and hollow. Bending her head, she followed the path of her hands with her lips. Her hair brushed across his chest as her mouth captured one nipple. His groan pleased and excited her. She raised her eyes, smiling at him, teasing him as her fingers slid lower.

"You are putting matches to dry wood," he warned, watching her, loving the feel of her touch and the bold way she moved over him. She offered him trust with every move. His hands settled on her shoulders, pulling her up his body so that he could have her mouth.

Ben drove forward meeting thrust for thrust. Cinnamon surged beneath him, twisting, arching, her body a living challenge to the man who would bind her with passion and desire. Ben took all that she gave and returned it tenfold. This was no tender mating, no gentle loving. The world was going up in flames. Higher he reached, the sweat pouring off his body, just feeding the fire. Cinnamon writhed, her breath coming in gasps as release hovered before her. With a cry echoed by Ben, she pushed with her dwindling strength one final time, tipping over the edge. Held close to each other, they tumbled from the peak into the silence that remained.

Ben raised himself on his elbow looking down into Cinnamon's eyes. They were still joined as one, his flesh to hers. Her heat shared with his. Her scent was all around him, the fragrance of their lovemaking rich in the stillness.

There were so many words he wanted to say, words he didn't even know the meaning of. But the time was not right. Cinnamon had given him more of herself than he suspected she knew. He wanted no cause for her to regret her trust. Even now he could feel his tension ease.

"You're beautiful," he whispered, as she continued to look at him without speaking.

"We are beautiful together," she corrected, relaxing again. She smiled slightly, arching a little. The sudden flexing of his body widened her grin. "So soon?" she whispered, delighted to know his need was as great as her own. The first joining had been but an appetizer. She wanted more.

"I thought I was being considerate," he murmured, dipping his head to tease one erect rosy peak. "I let you catch your breath."

"You're all heart—" her hands slid over his back, kneading his muscles, finding all the spots that gave him pleasure "—and a few other things, as well," she added, as his teeth lightly grazed her nipple. She gasped, the heat of passion building again.

Ben thrust smoothly, slowly, deeply, drawing out each stroke. Her body rose to meet his, joining him in the erotic dance. The fire burned more slowly, longer. The flames rose higher brighter with each movement. Her gasps matched his. Her body flowed around him, drawing every last ounce of strength as he made the final push to carry them to the source of fulfillment. Her name was on his lips as he collapsed over her, shielding her, finding shelter in the soft haven of her body.

His name was in the trembling whisper as Cinnamon found her own release in his arms. She fell asleep as she lay, trusting him enough to remain intimately connected and vulnerable. He rolled on his side and drew the covers over their bodies before allowing sleep to claim him, too.

Eight

Cinnamon pulled Ben's robe around her as she stood at the window and stared out over the city. Suddenly she had committed herself to someone. She glanced back at the bed where Ben slept. She didn't regret her choice, but she now had to look at the long-range results of her actions. She was having a relationship with one of the security men of a hopeful presidential candidate. If their affair became common knowledge, she could ruin Ben's career and, if not ruin her own, damage it. She should have been running away from Ben as far and as fast as she could. Instead she was standing here trying to figure out how to have Ben and protect them both. Nothing was impossible. She had learned that lesson well. Only the wanting mattered. If you wanted anything hard enough you could make the impossible a certainty. She wanted Ben. She would make the rest work.

"Thinking or regretting?" Ben asked quietly.

Cinnamon turned, smiling slightly, her eyes bright with memories. "Never regretting." She walked over to him.

Ben watched her, enjoying the smooth way she moved. Even cocooned in his robe, nothing could diminish her presence or her grace. "I'm glad." He reached for the tie and tugged it free. Her skin glowed softly in the early-morning light. There were faint marks from his beard on her body. He touched one lightly. "I'm sorry. Does it hurt?"

Cinnamon threaded her fingers through his hair. "Not at all. Tender, only. I like the feeling. It's like pinching yourself to make sure the reality isn't a dream."

He lifted his head, his lips level with the tips of her breasts. Blowing gently, he teased her, his eyes gleaming at the soft moan as she arched nearer. "Did you have fun, darling?"

"You know I did." Her fingers marched down his chest, pulling at the soft hair before tangling in the mat to scrape lightly over his nipples. "Don't play games, my friend. I'm hungry."

"For what?" he demanded huskily, drawing her down beside him.

"You need a diagram?" Her brows arched as she lay beside him, twisting to allow him the freedom to stroke her. Neither of them was serious yet, but they soon would be. She liked the playful enjoyment of this time almost as much as she liked feeling Ben inside of her just before he drove them over the edge of madness.

"Woman, you're insatiable."

"The pot calling the kettle black."

Ben raised up on one elbow. "Open your mouth and kiss me before I do one of us an injury."

Cinnamon laughed, her humor slipping away as he joined them as one.

Ben flexed his fingers against the steering wheel as he guided his car away from Cinnamon's apartment. In less than six hours they would board a plane for New Hampshire. Discretion would be their watchword. Cinnamon had made that clear. He frowned, remembering her awkwardness as she had tried to explain that they could not be open about their relationship. For some reason it hadn't occurred to her that he would want the same things as she. Somehow she seemed to think he would flaunt his presence. He couldn't help wondering if this were not another example of how she expected the people in her life to let her down or use her. He didn't like the feeling, especially when her reaction was so close to the truth.

"Damn Jonathon," he swore with feeling.

By rights he should report the latest development in Cinnamon's past. He knew he wouldn't. There were other ways to find out if his idea was a bunch of farfetched nonsense or a reality. He wanted to believe that the incongruities in Cinnamon's past were the result of the overlay of the real identity and the alias and not due to a monstrous plot to be the power behind the president. He knew Jonathon and his superiors wouldn't listen to him without more proof than his gut instinct.

"So I'll get the evidence."

But first he had to find out who Cinnamon had been before she became "Cinnamon Cartier." He had a trusted friend in the agency who could do a background search on anyone being investigated. Although this standard procedure had already been taken care of, Ben wanted a second check. Four hours later, Ben faced the man seated at the computer keyboard, scowling at the answers he had received.

"Are you sure?"

"I'm telling you I can't find anything yet. Name changes are a bit tricky, depending on the state and the reasons for seeking the change. You don't seem to think this woman had a criminal record nor much of work record. Nor the money for a car so hence no driver's license. All of those would have required documentation. We checked her entrance into college. Everything there was fine. Primary and secondary-school records, birth certificate—the whole bit. Are you sure this is an alias? It looks to me as if this Cinnamon Cartier might just be the real thing or her paperwork was done by a damn good pro."

"I don't want to hear this. I thought these computers were supposed to be the next best thing to Big Brother."

"You can't get out what you don't put in." The operator shrugged. "I can keep checking but don't expect much."

Ben glared at the machine. He had been so sure. It was unlike him to be so far off. Had being with Cinnamon blinded him to the truth, destroyed his effectiveness? he wondered as he left the building. He had to go home to pack. He still had time. Jonathon had made it clear he wanted Cinnamon either neutralized or cleared before the first primary. Two weeks. Fourteen short days.

"You're really quiet. Something wrong?" Cinnamon asked. She had a plane window seat. The only way she tolerated flying was to look down at the passing scenery and forget she was in a fragile craft in the air. Today she discovered a second diversion. Ben's silent presence called to her senses, reminding her of their shared passion.

"Nothing. Just thinking about work." He searched her face, looking for a hint of uneasiness or that guarded look that she seemed to wear in public, which might tell that she was lying. The latter was visible when she spoke to the stewardess and when they had been accosted in the airport by a very enterprising reporter, but it was not there now. Her eyes were steady, and there was a faint softness in her gaze as she gazed at him. She couldn't look at him that way and lie. His instinct couldn't be that gummed up.

"You're staring," Cinnamon murmured, wondering at the searching glance. "You've been acting strangely since you picked me up. Care to tell me about it? Is it Don or his family?"

"Just thinking. Nothing important, really." He tried a shrug.

Cinnamon studied him for a moment longer. "You aren't regretting . . . ?"

Ben shook his head before she could finish. He took her hand, squeezing it tightly. "Don't be a fool." The words were a croon, an endearment.

Cinnamon smiled slightly. "Dumb question."

"You know it was. The only thing I'm regretting is our need to hide what we are to each other. I've discovered I have more of a stallion's pride over the best mare in the herd than I thought."

Another woman might have been put off by such a description. Cinnamon laughed. "But, remember, it was the rogue mare that usually led the group. Her offspring were smarter, quicker and faster than the rest. She and the stallion created the strain that could survive anything, even man's encroachment on their homeland.''

His brows rose at the knowledge she displayed. ''For a city woman, you know a lot about the 'mustang concept.' ''

''I'm curious by nature. I like things that beat the odds. Mustangs do.'' She pulled her hand from his. It was risky to sit, hands linked, where anyone could see. The flight attendant was already watching Ben, liking what she saw. Her interest would make her sensitive to another woman's influence.

Ben frowned at the way she had moved away. He wanted to keep the contact. The same need he felt was in her eyes. He silently damned the assignment, Metcalf, the campaign and Jonathon. When this was all over, he was going to take Cinnamon to a place far away from everyone and spend the days and nights locked in her arms. He would know her every secret as she would know his.

But first, he had to clear up her background. He glanced around, making sure that the area was really as sparsely booked as it had appeared when they boarded. The seats behind and in front of them were unoccupied and the three rows across only had four people, two of which were reading. One was asleep and the other appeared to be working. No one to listen.

He looked back at Cinnamon. She was staring out the window again. ''What do you see out there?''

''Land, people, dreams—and no ugliness. It looks so pretty from here. If you flew over Chicago right now, it would seem like a postcard picture. You wouldn't see the slums, the homeless, the torn-up streets, the gangs or the graffiti." She pulled her gaze from the window to look at him. "What do you see?"

"Not nearly as much as you," he admitted, fascinated by her description. "For a cynic, you sound remarkably romantic. Why?"

"I've seen enough ugliness to last me a lifetime. I've been cold, hungry and at the end of my rope. Defeat is the bitterest taste in the world. And being cold all the way to your bones—so cold even a fire won't warm you—is a feeling you never forget. Hunger isn't nearly as bad, in spite of what people would have you believe." She glanced back to the window. "I prefer where I am now. I'll never go back."

"Why would you worry about something like that? You're well on your way to establishing yourself."

Her lips curved into a bitter smile. "In an arena where the bull has more rights than I do. Where his life and lot is assured and mine is constantly on the line. One misstep. A word wrong. A rumor. A truth that was the only decision one could make in past circumstances judged against a new reality can destroy my career. It has been done to others more powerful than I."

Ben's instincts went to alert. Facts. She was working from facts, not supposition. Her past was closer. He could feel it. "What truth could destroy you? Let me help you." His feelings for her overshadowed his caution.

Cinnamon stiffened, wary, angry at herself for allowing her guard to drop so completely. "I don't know what you're talking about." She forced herself to meet his eyes.

Ben cursed himself, even as he tried to find a way to redeem the situation. She was suspicious, sensing a trap. He hated the look in her eyes. "You know I wondered how you could put yourself through college, given your background. Did you get a scholarship?"

"Wasn't that in my dossier?" How could she have forgotten his role in her life? How could she have been so blinded by passion to lose sight of the danger he represented? Then a more horrifying thought occurred. Just how far back did that dossier extend? She knew that with Don and the family, it went back to the year one. But what about hers? She couldn't think of a way of asking without arousing suspicion. All the times that truth and lies had merged came back to haunt her.

She stared at Ben. He didn't seem suspicious, only curious. She relaxed slightly, promising herself to be more careful. She had taken enough chances.

"All right. So I know you didn't get any assistance. But the question still stands."

"I worked for it. What did you think? I stole it?" Hurt, angry, confused by the tumble of emotions his probing had unleashed she resorted to sarcasm.

"You were twenty when you started."

"And I finished in three years. It's all I had the money for."

"Then you started to work for Metcalf for peanuts."

"I have managed on less." She turned back to the window, meaning to end the conversation.

Ben stared at her averted profile. Resistance was in every line of her body. He wanted to pull her into his arms and tell her that if she would give him the truth, he could make it work—whatever it was. He sighed, running his fingers through his hair. He hated working blind. Damn Jonathon for his suspicions. Damn Cinnamon for being so wary that she couldn't trust him. And damn himself for the lies he had told and would keep on telling to buy the truth. How would he explain when this was over?

"Don't shut me out," he pleaded for the man not the professional.

Cinnamon didn't look at him. His voice was already stealing away her resolve. No one had ever really cared about her. No one had ever wanted so much from her. She didn't believe in happily-ever-afters. Ben would go, one day. She still had to survive. Giving him so much of herself lessened her chances.

"Don't keep pushing. We only sleep together. I don't owe you the story of my life." The words were more than a demand. They were a plea born of fear and bewilderment.

Ben fought his temper on hearing her description of their lovemaking. True, there had been no promises, no words of love but their joining had had more meaning than sleeping together. "How about a trade? I'll tell you mine."

"I'm not interested." She shrugged, delivering the lie with more indifference than she felt.

"You're a liar. A woman like you doesn't 'sleep with' a man lightly. You want to know all right but you don't want me to share any part of your life in return. No ties. Is that how it goes?"

The bitter question whipped her conscience. She turned, glaring at him. Her anger died when she saw the pain in his eyes. He had reached past her guard and touched her heart. "I worked as a waitress, I told you that. I got paid under the table by a slimy little man in a dinky town somewhere between Chicago and Knoxville who was more interested in having a sexy pair of legs to handle his ribald clientele than he was in the fact that I was obviously underage."

Another human to add to the list of those who had taught Cinnamon not to trust, to believe. "Bars are inspected by the liquor-licensing people."

"Big deal. There are such things as bribes, but in this case we knew the inspector. Every time he came in I simply went in the bathroom while the other girls covered for me. In spite of the place, I met people there that I could like. In a way that bar was the reason I thought about politics." Meaning only to answer his one question, she found that once she was started, she wanted him to understand. "The mayor would come in every now and then. He was nice, soft-spoken, always well turned out. I know now he was nothing more than a small-town politician, but to me he looked the epitome of elegance and power." She smiled a little at her own naiveté. "You have to remember, I had nothing to compare him with. He even dated my friend, Cin..." She covered a cough, then finished the name. "Cindy."

"He loaned me some books, even recommended a school. I was sixteen-and-a-half at the time. I know now that he was only humoring me—then I believed the dream was possible, so I made the impossible true. It took four years to save up. And even then I wouldn't have enough if my friend hadn't given me her savings to add to the pot." Cinnamon paused, remembering how her friend had given her the money. She had willed it to Cinnamon on her deathbed, complete with witnesses. She had also given her something even more valuable, but that she couldn't tell Ben.

Ben frowned, disturbed by the story, not just for the sadness of the life she had led, but because he sensed the most important points had been left out. "If your friend was in the same situation as you, how could she afford to do that?"

She should have known he would find the weak spots in her tale. "She had no more use for money."

"She found a man to support her?"

Cinnamon looked down at her hands, surprised to find them clinched in her lap. "No. She was run down by a drunk on her way home from work one night. The horror of it was she was working my shift. I had the flu." The tears stung her eyes at the words she had never said out loud.

Ben covered her hands with his when the first drop splashed down on his skin. Once, he had lain in a stinky Third World prison, battered by guards and half fried by fever. He'd hurt less than he did now watching her weep those silent tears. "Don't you dare cry here where I can't hold you," he commanded fiercely.

Cinnamon lifted her head, her eyes glittering with temper and pain. "You wouldn't leave it alone."

He couldn't take the pain from her memories but he could give her a target for her anger. "So I'm a nosy fool. Sue me." He shrugged, baiting her.

"I'd rather slap your face," she snapped, the tears drying.

"All right. I guess I owe you that. Tonight, if you like." Ben masked his relief on seeing the sadness leave her face. She was back in fighting form and he had some of his answers. All that remained was to find out where Cinnamon had gotten her name. The last piece of hard evidence to get Jonathon off their backs and out of her life.

Ben glared at the message in his hand. It had been waiting for him when he checked in. Codes. He'd had enough of them to last a lifetime. This one, when translated, said "Call Jonathon, private number, ASAP." Reaching for the phone beside the bed he dialed the safe line and waited. Jonathon's precise voice answered coolly.

"What's up?"

"I might ask you the same thing. I thought I made myself clear. I wished to be kept informed on the Cartier case. I understand you made an unauthorized records search. What made you doubt the validity of our initial search? Or were you looking for something more specific?"

"You know this spy business is a real pain in the tail when I find out that even I am being watched. Don't you ever get tired of bird-dogging my rear?"

"The facts, Forsythe. I am not in the mood for your infantile temperament. The ones who instigated this research project are getting most restless."

"Then let them get out here and do the work. It takes time to establish a level of communication and a certain amount of trust."

"I know what kind of trust you're talking about. It better bring results."

Distaste was thick in Jonathon's voice. Ben controlled his temper, knowing he would be playing right into Jonathon's hands by objecting to the man's hints about any intimacy between him and Cinnamon.

"I don't like you and I don't like what I'm doing. But listen to me. I will finish this case and you'll have your ends all tied up in a neat little bow. But I'll do it my way."

"Time's growing short. Metcalf arrives in New Hampshire a week from today."

"I know that."

"But—"

"No, buts. I'm doing the job you sent me to do. That's all you're getting out of me now." Ben slammed down the phone and paced to the window. He didn't like knowing that his relationship with Cinnamon was an open book. He didn't like knowing he wanted to protect her but couldn't yet. He didn't like knowing that he used her feelings for him in order to get the answers he needed. But more than anything else, he didn't like himself.

"Honey, you deserve more than an openhanded swing at my face for this one," he murmured aloud to the empty room. "I just hope you're going to give me a chance to let you get even when this is all over."

Cinnamon put the finishing touches on her make-up just as Ben knocked on her door. She let him in. "I'm almost ready. Did you get your business taken care of?" she asked as she collected her briefcase.

Ben watched her, for one moment wishing he could bundle her on a plane and escape the whole setup. All Jonathon wanted was her out of the way. To him, one way was as good as another. "I did."

"You don't sound too happy about it." She glanced over her shoulder, catching his frown.

"I have a rule-follower boss who seems intent on making my life miserable," he admitted irritably. "I guess that's one reason I'm getting out soon."

Startled, Cinnamon stared at him. "What do you mean getting out?"

"I'm technically out of work as of the end of next week." There was no point in not telling her.

"Oh." Cinnamon absorbed the news, shocked to realize she hadn't looked even that far into the future. She had known she wouldn't always have Ben. No one ever stayed in her life for long. But this time, she hadn't expected so short a term. "Then what?" she made herself ask.

"Don't know for sure. I haven't had a real vacation for years. I thought I'd knock around for a while and then make up my mind. Care to come along?" He tossed the suggestion out, trying to sound casual.

Cinnamon turned away and headed for the door. She didn't want to acknowledge that for once in her life she was tempted to toss aside her own plans. "You know I can't—the campaign."

Ben followed, knowing his feelings of disappointment at her quick response was illogical. "And when that's over? Then what?"

"I don't understand." She sent him a bewildered look. "I work for Don, whether it's an election year or not."

"What about your private life?"

"What about it?"

"Better yet, what about us?"

Cinnamon couldn't look at him and say the words. "There is no 'us' except for now."

"Is that all you want from me?"

His line of questioning was way off, but he couldn't stop. He wasn't even sure what he wanted her to say.

Cinnamon turned and leaned against the door, feeling cornered. "I don't know what you want me to say. I want you, but you never said anything about ties. Neither did I. I never thought of it for either of us."

Ben placed his hands against the door so that she was trapped between it and him. "And if I *did* want ties? Would you run?"

"Don't ask hypothetical questions. We both deal in facts. Either cut bait or fish," she snapped.

"All right. I don't want to let you go. Plain enough?"

"And?"

"And come with me. Now. Tonight!"

"No!" Cinnamon shook her head, fighting him and herself. The door was hard against her skin as she tried to press away from his warmth. "I won't live hand to mouth, ever again. I told you that."

"I can take care of you."

"I don't *want* anyone to take care of me. I can do that. You're asking me to give up everything I've worked for. I won't. I can't."

"You love the power," he corrected angrily.

The attack was unexpected. "I don't know what you're talking about."

"You know. I've watched you in action. You twirl people around on a string. Oh, I'll grant you they like it and you never pull the string tight enough to hurt them and you always make sure they get what they want. But you are in control."

Appalled by his assessment, Cinnamon stared at him. It was a measure of how close she had allowed

him to get to her that she could feel the hurt straight
to her heart. "You're crazy."

"Why? Because I see you for what you are, and care
about you anyway. I didn't have any choice, woman.
I took one look and I was lost." He bent his head and
took her lips, not even noticing she tried to resist him.
For the first time he didn't kiss her to give pleasure but
to prove to her and himself that he could take what she
could give and more. When he raised his head, her
eyes held passion and knowledge. He took her briefcase from her lax fingers, cupped her elbow and
opened the door.

"Think on that awhile. Find an answer," he commanded as he urged her into the corridor.

Nine

Cinnamon couldn't relax, couldn't lose herself in the controlled chaos going on around her. The campaign headquarters was alive with energy, optimism and chatter. A hundred details awaited her personal attention. Any one of them should have fired her blood and brought a pleasurable surge of adrenaline to a head. Instead, she was nervy, tense and wary. Every time she smiled at someone, spoke or gave a direction she could feel Ben's eyes on her, see the look that said he remembered what he had told her even if she wouldn't.

Power. Yes, she loved it, courted it and used it. But Ben had made her sound like one of those political generals that couldn't tell right from wrong, one of the breed who bent the rules to get the candidate elected. Yes, she played the game but she was honest. She hated lies. The one she lived was enough.

"Ms. Cartier. These are the printer's proofs you asked to see."

The youthful voice of one of the workers broke into her thoughts. Cinnamon pulled herself together enough to smile at the young girl and take the folder she held. "Thank you, Mary."

"I know you're busy and all." Mary shifted nervously from foot to foot. "But I just wanted to tell you how much I admire you. Senator Metcalf is a good man, and I know he'll make a good president. But it's you who'll make it possible. I'm taking political science in college. One day I want to be like you." She gave a half smile, hesitant, shy but determined.

Cinnamon looked into her face and saw the unrealized dreams. Maybe Mary would succeed, but Cinnamon doubted it. She was too soft; the hunger for success just wasn't there. Mary clearly came from a caring family, a protective environment. Her chances of surviving in Cinnamon's world were almost nil.

"You have to want it more than anything," she warned, doing something she wouldn't have considered doing before Ben's entrance into her life. She never offered advice when it hadn't been asked. She'd never wanted to risk rejection from a stranger.

"Oh, I do. It's so exciting isn't it?" Mary's eyes shone as she glanced around the room.

Cinnamon felt her age and experience showing against the bubbling enthusiasm of the younger woman's look. And suddenly, she wanted Mary gone. "I need to get these done."

Mary cast her apologetic look. "I'm sorry," she stammered before hurrying away.

Ben watched that small exchange from across the room. Supposedly, he was checking on the layout of the building where they would hold a small campaign workers' reception the evening Metcalf arrived. It hadn't taken him more than a few minutes to make the necessary inspection. Now he had time to study Cinnamon in action. She wasn't the woman he had seen on videotapes. She was on edge, distracted and off-balance. He doubted anyone else noticed, but he knew her better than most. There was a frown between those lovely eyes, a tightness in her movements that hadn't been there yesterday. He was almost sure she was remembering what he had said. For a moment he wondered if he had been too brutal, then shook his head. He had to stop her, for her sake and his own. He wanted more than today and tomorrow with her: he wanted forever.

Falling in love. To him it had been a phrase, a buzz word for the foolish state of man-woman relationship. He knew what love was, had felt the emotion for some of the people in his life, even for one woman, his former partner Suzanne. But the feeling had been different. He would have stepped in front of a bullet to protect Suzanne, but her tears would never have made him feel as if his heart had been torn from his body. He would never have tried to influence Suzanne's life or make a place for himself there. He had never desired Suzanne as a woman—only as a friend, a partner and maybe the sister he had never had. That was love to him. Loyalty. Caring. Sacrifice, if necessary. But not this gut-wrenching pain that demanded release from its cage. Not this fire that consumed only to feed an even greater fire. Not this need to shelter, to protect, even if the love was given to one who had done wrong, who had broken laws. He would prove Cinnamon innocent because he sincerely believed she

He needed her taste more than he needed his next breath.

Cinnamon threaded her fingers through his hair when their lips met. She drank of him, slaking her thirst, demanding his strength and passion. "I want you," she whispered against his mouth. "I want to burn with you. I want to watch you burn with me."

She tangled her legs with his, feeling his thighs contract to hold her in place. "Teach me how to please you."

"Please me anymore and I'll die from it," he groaned as her hands found the source of the sweetest pain he had ever known.

She painted the erotic pictures in her mind with words and motion. Ben returned her whispers with deep groans, arching against her hands until she couldn't think, taste or smell anything but him.

He was hers.

"I want you. All of you." She pulled him to her, trying to guide him toward the entry they both craved.

Ben rolled her over in one smooth surge of power. "Not so fast," he commanded, taking control.

Cinnamon gazed up at him, her eyes gleamed with challenge, daring him to take her, inviting him to touch her as deeply as she touched him.

He smiled at the look and courage of the woman who burned in his arms. "Fire in your hair and fire in your heart," he breathed, sheathing himself in her.

She laughed, glorying in the possession even as she moved to bind him to her, her hips lifting and tightening around him. "You're the storm. And I love storms." Her words were little more than whispered gasps as the pleasure built to the edge of pain.

"Firestorm." A prayer or a benediction?

was. But he would have taken her even had she been as guilty as the first sin of mankind.

Ben stared across the room, catching her gaze. She was hurting, and he had done it. She would hurt more soon, for he had to tell her the truth before they could make plans for the future. He frowned. He had to make arrangements for their future, if only short-term ones. He needed time and space to heal the damage that would be done when she realized who he was and why he had sought her out. He had no illusions. He was betraying her, and she would see it no other way. But that, too, didn't matter. One day, no matter how long it took, he would win.

"Tired?" Ben glanced at Cinnamon as she curled on her side of the rented car. She hadn't said much since they had left the campaign headquarters. "It's been a long day. I had no idea when we got up this morning that it wouldn't end until ten. I don't know where you get the energy to do this every day. Or does it get better?" He talked hoping to draw her out.

"It won't." Cinnamon didn't look at him; instead she gazed out the window at the snow-shrouded landscape. One thing she could say for New Hampshire, it was prepared for snow conditions. Unlike Washington, where an inch of powder could paralyze the town, here roads were cleared, the phones and the plumbing worked.

"Talk to me, Cinnamon. Call me a rat if that will make you feel any better," Ben said with a sigh.

"I'm too tired to talk, and there really isn't anything to say. You have your opinion."

"But? There is a but, isn't there?"

"You're right."

He frowned at the flat response. "That's all you're going to say?"

Cinnamon stirred slightly, almost giving in to the urge to look at him. "What do you want me to say? That I need to be in control? That it makes me feel safe?" The anger smoldered but she didn't let it out. She hadn't wanted Ben to hold a mirror up to her so that she had to see what she had become. She didn't even know why he had or why he cared. More than that, she was afraid to ask.

"So what are you going to do about it?"

"Nothing."

Ben's hands clenched on the steering wheel. "You can't mean that."

She turned then, glaring at him. "I've come too far to turn back even if I wanted to. This is all I know."

"You could learn more." In spite of his best efforts, frustration was seeping into his voice.

"Stop pushing me," Cinnamon shouted, suddenly driven to the end of her rope. "You have no right."

"I do. You gave it to me when we slept together. Or are you going to tell me that all I got was your body?"

Ben eased the car off the road, into a deserted parking lot. The moment the vehicle stopped, Cinnamon was out of the car and striding into the darkness. Ben was right behind her. Neither noticed the cold, the lack of moonlight, or the silence.

Ben caught her arm, swinging her around to face him. Cinnamon's hand flew up. Only Ben's own sharply honed instincts saved him from the full force of the closed hand aimed at his jaw. He grabbed her wrist, trapping it against his body as she fought him. Then it was over. Cinnamon slumped against his chest, her tears falling to drench the front of his coat.

"Damn you. Why couldn't you leave me alone? I was fine until you pushed your way into my life," she cried.

Ben pulled her close, absorbing her pain, sheltering her from the wind. He lifted her in his arms, half expecting her to struggle. When she only wound her arms around his neck and pressed closer, he sighed deeply. He carried her to the car and got in on the passenger side so that she ended up in his lap.

He held her, stroking her hair as she wept against him. He didn't completely understand what the cause of the outburst was, but he would not ask now.

Cinnamon cried until there were no more tears. She hadn't meant to swing at Ben—hadn't known that she still remembered how to protect herself. It had been so long since she had needed the skill.

"I'm sorry," she whispered, when she could talk.

"No. I am." Ben laid his cheek against her hair, his arms tightening around her. He wanted to say I love you but couldn't. Not until he could tell her the whole truth. That was one humiliation, one misunderstanding he could save her.

"I hurt you."

"You told the truth." She lifted her head. "No one cared enough to say it." She reached out, her fingers brushing his lips, tracing the fullness that had given her such pleasure.

Ben kissed her fingers, discovering a new meaning to the word *pain*. He didn't have to see her eyes to know that trust was burning there. Desire was a slow burn in his blood. He wanted her, but more than that, he wanted to protect her from anything or anyone who might harm her. "What are you going to do?"

Cinnamon lifted her lips to his, needing his taste to drive out the uncertainty. He made the world right because he held her. In some strange way, he filled all the empty places in her life. Honesty was easy, sometimes frighteningly so. "I don't know. I don't know how to stop. I don't know if I even want to." She leaned her head against his chest, needing the feel of him surrounding her. "Nothing I've done seems right any more."

Ben tipped her head against his shoulder, one hand settling, cupping her breast. Her heart beat strongly beneath his touch. "Then start over with me." Urgency drove him. A need to get her away. He didn't question the instinct. He simply obeyed it. "Say the word, and we can leave tonight."

Cinnamon stared into his eyes, seeing desperation there and something more. Her body was responding to its mate. The past was far away, without pain, without the driving ambition that had dogged her footsteps for so long. She wanted him. "You'd do that for me?" No one in her life but one person had ever really offered her anything without strings or payment.

"I'd do that for us. We belong together, you and I. Your strength to mine. Our needs mesh. Trust me. Trust yourself." He wanted to force her to agree but knew he couldn't. It had to be her choice or nothing. But there was nothing that said he couldn't stack the deck in his favor. He bent his head, taking her lips, putting every word he could not say into the kiss he gave her.

Her tongue met his, taking and demanding in turn. Her body twisted in his hands as he stroked the full curve of her breast. Her moan was a sweet sound, filling the car with unleashed passion. The buttons of her blouse parted, giving him access to the living warmth of her skin. Cinnamon pressed her breasts against him, feeling the heat build.

"I want to say yes," she whispered, torn as she had never been before. "I want you so much. You make me feel whole."

"Then come with me."

Their eyes met. He knew before she spoke that he had lost.

"I can't." The agony of her decision was in her eyes and in her voice. "I must finish what I started. Ask me again at the end of the campaign—if you still want me."

Ben had lived long enough to know prayers weren't always answered. The drama was drawing to a close. He could feel it. Sometime in the next few weeks he would look back and know he should have taken her tonight, and damn the consequences. He would also look back and know as he knew now he had no choice. The cards had already been dealt.

"All right." He bent his head and took her lips, feeding on her passion as she fed on his. This was all that bound them, in Cinnamon's eyes. He had to tighten the bonds as much as he could. His overwhelming desire might be the only protection he would be able to offer her in the end. She might see his words or actions as betrayals, but she would never be able to doubt that he had wanted her.

Cinnamon entered her hotel room, weary and yet relaxed. Being with Ben tonight had been all she had needed. A small smile touched her lips. In a car. It was a wonder either of them could move. But she had needed him so much—needed his passion and his possession. He had given her more than she asked, touching her with an urgency that was contagious, even if she didn't understand it. Now she was alone. Ben was in his room alone, as well. Was his bed as cold as hers looked? She frowned upon seeing the message light on the phone. It had to be Don. A moment later she paled on hearing the desk clerk read the six words from her past.

"Ellen, baby, I miss you. Mother."

"Did you see the person who left this?" she asked trying to speak calmly. All these years she had thought her mother dead. To know the lie was a shock beyond anything that had gone before. Her hands shook as they gripped the phone.

"I'm sorry. But I had stepped away from the desk for a moment. The message was lying here when I returned."

Cinnamon managed to thank the clerk before hanging up the phone. She had to think. How and where had the lie begun? Her mother or someone else? She didn't know. The answer was lost somewhere in the mists of the past. Now she had no choice. She had to deal with the present. She could not let her parent endanger the campaign or the life she had built for herself. She had come too far, risked too much and worked too hard to lose everything now.

The phone rang. Cinnamon stared at it, mesmerized. Five minutes ago she wouldn't have hesitated about picking it up. Now she was scared. All the emotions of the child who had suffered in silence came rushing back. The metallic taste of fear was in her mouth as she reached for the receiver.

"Ellen. I want to see you, baby."

The words made her shake. The croon hadn't changed.

Cinnamon slammed down the phone, wrapping her arms around herself and rocking back and forth. Five minutes later, it rang again. She couldn't answer. She could make herself touch the instrument to stop the ringing. Tears streamed down her cheeks, but she didn't notice. How had her mother found her? Then she remembered. The reporter in the airport this morning. A candid picture. She hadn't been prepared. Her hair had been hanging down her back because Ben had liked it that way. She had wanted to please him. She had forgotten it had been mother's favorite hairstyle for her in her teens.

A knock on her door startled her. She jumped, automatically cringing.

"Cinnamon, let me in. Cinnamon?" Ben rapped again, worried at the silence and the fact Cinnamon hadn't answered her phone.

Cinnamon forced her muscles to unlock. She had to reply before Ben took the door off the hinges. "I'm coming."

Ben hooked his thumbs in his belt, not liking the strained tone of her voice. Something was wrong. One look at the pale face that peered cautiously around the crack in the door was enough to make him revise his assessment. Something was terribly wrong.

"Honey, what is it?" He demanded, kicking the door shut as soon as he was inside.

Cinnamon tried a smile as she attempted to think of an explanation that would satisfy him. "A rather nasty caller. I get them from time to time. I just never seem to get used to it."

He stared at her unable to believe she would try such a blatant a lie. He started to call her on it when the phone rang. The flash of terror in her eyes made him grab the receiver.

"Who the devil is this?" he barked. The muted click of the broken connection made him swear long and hard.

Cinnamon sat down, her legs too weak to support her. "I told you." She had to stop shaking or he never would leave. She needed to be alone, to think, to figure out her mother's next move. She wasn't a child to be intimidated any longer. There were choices now she hadn't had then.

Ben sat down beside her on the bed. "Let me help you. Tell me what's wrong. You aren't the kind of woman to go to pieces at an obscene phone call."

Cinnamon shook her head, resisting his urgent plea. She wanted to lean on him, let him take care of her problems, let him protect her from her mother. But she didn't dare. What if he turned away? How would she survive? Taking a deep breath, she forced some strength to her limbs, calm to her voice. "I'll deal with it. It's my problem. No one else's."

Ben studied her, wishing he dared push. She looked too pale. Her composure was paper thin. One wrong word could send her away from him. Her trust was such a new thing, too tender to stand much strain. "Then let me hold you," he whispered, giving the only comfort he thought she might allow. "At least for a little while."

Cinnamon stared at him, unable to believe he had backed off. She could tell he hadn't wanted to and yet he had. Glancing at his arms as he held them open to her, she struggled with the habits of a lifetime.

"Trust me that much, at least," he whispered, afraid to move closer.

"Does it matter so much?" She lifted her eyes to his and read the answer in the cloudy depths. Cinnamon wasn't conscious of moving. All she knew was the safety and warmth she found in his arms. She tucked her head comfortably beneath his chin as she relaxed.

Ben let out his breath in a careful sigh. She had given him more than she knew. One more tie. One more hedge against the pain that he knew would come when he told her the truth. He prayed she would remember he hadn't taken from her that which she hadn't wanted to give; that he had denied himself for her; that he had tried to allow her the freedom to know him and believe in more than just what he did for a living. He wanted her understanding when the time came. He just hoped she would have it to give.

"Do you want me to have the desk route your calls to my room for the rest of the night? I can tell them you have a migraine or that you're working on something and don't want to be disturbed."

"I wish I could, but no matter what excuse you give the clerk and whoever he tells, is going to think there's some hanky-panky going on. We can't afford that."

"Then unplug the thing. You need some sleep. Worrying if this person is going to call back won't allow you to get any."

"I can't do that, either. Don might call. Or any one of a dozen others. I have to be available." Cinnamon lifted her head, finally able to smile a little. "Don't sound so fierce. I'm all right, really." And in an odd way she was, too. The shakes and the fear had been lost in his arms. He had given her strength. The feeling was new. She wanted to thank him but didn't know how. Touching his face, she attempted to smooth the frown from between his brows.

Ben's hold tightened. "I like it when you touch me," he whispered, reading the beginning of passion in her eyes. He could feel his own building with the slow stroke of her fingers. "But don't tease. Not right now. I can't promise you that I have any control."

Cinnamon laughed brokenly. "I don't think I have any, either. I shouldn't be, but I want you. Now. I think I need you and I've never told that to anyone." She held her breath as she made the admission. For the first time in her life she was risking being vulnerable.

"Do you, honey?" Ben made himself speak through the lump in his throat. He could only imagine the courage her confession had taken. "You can't want me half as much as I want you." He caught the fingers tracing his lips between his teeth and nipped gently.

Cinnamon groaned softly. "I was hoping you would be strong."

"Little liar." He bent his head, tasting her mouth as his hands found and cupped her breasts. Leaning back, he sprawled on the bed, taking her with him.

Looking down at him, Cinnamon searched his eyes. "You make me feel—" She shook her head, trying to sort through the multitude of emotions within. "I can't explain it. I thought I understood myself. I was wrong. I feel things with you that frighten me." Her hands framed his face, seeking the answers in his expression. "Sometimes I think you know something I don't. And if I just look long enough I'll find the answer. Only I don't. I get confused. I want to please you. I try. I don't even know why."

Ben could have told her. He knew her feelings because they paralleled his own. He knew, too, she had to find her own way. She might not be able to commit herself to him. Her life had created her, and it also could destroy their relationship, no matter what the emotions involved were. Happily-ever-after didn't always happen in real life.

"You please me very much," he whispered, giving her the only reassurance he could. "More than any other." He tucked a strand of fiery hair behind her ear. "Do you want me to stay?"

"More than I can tell you. But you can't." Her eyes darkened with regret. "I would have liked to fall asleep with you."

Ben felt his body's instant response. He ignored it and the pain it brought. He took her mouth instead. The kiss wasn't enough. She trembled against him as he lifted her away. "I either leave now or I don't leave at all. Help me."

Cinnamon relaxed against him for one moment then slipped off him to stand beside the bed. Her legs felt like jelly and her hands were shaking. And she didn't mind at all that he could see what he did to her. For she could see some of the same reactions in Ben. She took the hand he held out and walked with him to the door.

"Call me if you get any more of those things. We'll go for a walk in full view of the town if we must so that you don't have to sit here waiting for that phone to ring."

Cinnamon smiled—tenderness, an emotion she had never known, welling within. "I don't know how much of a chaperon a sleeping town would be, especially on a moonless night."

"I'd find somewhere that had people." He leaned slightly to kiss her without touching anything more than her lips. His control was strained to the limit as it was. "Promise me," he commanded when he raised his head.

"I promise," she whispered.

Then he was gone and she was alone to face the past.

Ten

Cinnamon stretched slowly from the last yoga position before lying back out on the carpet to savor the peace the exercise had brought. She'd had a restless night even though there hadn't been any more annoying calls, so she needed all the help she could get to start the day. Dawn was just breaking through the clouds. The day promised to be cold but fair. The sky was blue. The campaign plans were going well. Don would be here soon. She frowned a little, remembering his most recent phone call. He hadn't sounded as eager as he should have. Obviously the week long break hadn't been as beneficial as she'd hoped. She knew Linda was tired of the unrelenting travel, although she never complained. She knew, too, that the twins found the need to be on guard a strain although they hadn't said anything. What worried her was that from now on the campaign would really go into high gear. Unless the pollsters were wrong, Don would take the New Hampshire primary. And history had written an interesting legend for the winner here. Of the last seven presidents, all had won the New Hampshire vote.

Cinnamon's frown deepened. Her mother. She had to keep her parent out of the limelight until she could find a way to neutralize her threat to the election. She knew without question that Don would stand behind her. He was that kind of man, loyal, willing to sacrifice himself for the underdog. Both their dreams were in jeopardy and she still didn't know how to protect either of them. And Ben? She had risked mixing her true background with the one that was probably in his dossier. Her slip had been the result of impulse and she hadn't been able to do anything about it. Now it was too late and the damage was done.

The phone rang. She started, staring at it. This time she didn't let the fear overwhelm her. She fought it back, reminding herself she was an adult now. Her mother couldn't hurt her anymore, not the way she had been hurt in the past. Rising, she lifted the receiver, exhaling slowly on recognizing Ben's voice.

"Ready for breakfast?"

"Give me ten minutes."

Ben paused then asked the question uppermost in his mind. "Did you sleep well?"

"Better than I expected. No surprises."

"Good. See you in ten minutes, honey."

Ben hung up and sat staring out the window. Cinnamon Cartier was or had been a real person. His brow furrowed at the errant thought. For a moment he examined it, then swore. Then he remembered the slip. One tiny cough. Had Cinnamon, when she had been relating the story of her time after she had run away, started to say Cinnamon instead of the name Cindy for her best friend? The one who had died in her place? The pieces would fit. The discrepancies would match. The slight variation in the fact that Cinnamon's mother hadn't died when she was four as was in the original dossier, had in fact been around to hurt her until at least age sixteen. It would also explain why, although Cinnamon was supposed to be thirty, she looked no more than in her late twenties. Facts. They had been there all the time, but he had been too close to see them.

Snatching the phone up, he punched out his records friend's home number. The groggy voice answered. Ben told him what he wanted.

"This time make sure Jonathon doesn't get wind of what I'm checking," he ordered sharply.

"I'll do my best," came the reply.

"Get back to me here. If I'm not in, don't leave a message. Anyone could pick it up. Just keep trying."

"Will do."

Ben hung up, beginning to feel as if he just might have an answer soon. But that still didn't explain last night. Who had Cinnamon running scared? And why? He couldn't protect her if he didn't know from which direction the threat came.

He glanced at his watch. The ten minutes were up. He would just have to stick close to her. Tail her, if necessary. He'd be there for her in spite of anything she tried to do. She'd learn to trust him completely one way or another.

* * *

"Are you sure you want to do this?" Cinnamon demanded, glancing at Ben as he patiently folded and stuffed envelopes.

He grinned. "No, I'm not sure I want to do this. I know I don't want to do this. But it's where you are so that's where I intend to be. And what could be more innocent?"

Ben looked around the busy room. Everyone had a job. Most of the Metcalf staff were talking in voices high with excitement and nervous energy. Phones were ringing constantly, people coming in and out of the room, regardless of the cold that swirled through the room with each passage. Donald Metcalf's picture covered every inch of space everywhere. And when the space was too small there was a button or bumper sticker plastered on the square. Even he had a pin stuck to his coat, courtesy of some cute little cheerleader type who had looked awestruck every time she glanced in Cinnamon's direction. A madhouse would have been an apt description. Ben wasn't sure his ears would ever be the same. He had been in shoot-outs that had created less noise and chaos.

"I don't know how you stand this. And like it from the looks of you."

Cinnamon chuckled before sobering. She was working on her own stack of envelopes. Technically, she didn't have to be involved with so mundane a chore. But the truth was her own work was done and she needed something to keep her busy. The past two days had been quiet. Not a peep from her mother. The strain of waiting for her to pounce was getting to Cinnamon. The nervousness had been a godsend in a way. She worked late into the night in an effort to tire herself enough to sleep and had managed to catch up on all the myriad details left for her personal attention. Now she realized she had time on her hands. Time she could have spent with Ben if the town hadn't taken to watching both of them every moment. Reporters were following them around. And if it wasn't the newspeople, it was some citizen or other giving their views on the political scene and demanding to know where Don stood. She had tried to take it all in stride. As little as a month ago, she would have thrived on the attention the campaign was generating. Not now.

"You're frowning again," Ben observed, knowing she was worrying about the calls. Although she had said nothing more about the calls, Cinnamon was tense and clearly worried. He had reached the conclusion, unpalatable though it was, that she knew the caller and expected the contact again.

"Am I?"

Cinnamon smiled, striving for the right note of casual interest. She knew Ben was watching her closely. He was always near now. Hovering but doing such a good job of it, she couldn't object unless she wanted to admit she saw more than he thought. So they both played the game.

"Penny for them."

"I was wondering where to eat lunch. I'm starved."

One of these days he would be realistic and stop hoping she would confide in him. Stifling his disappointment, he worked as hard as she at being casual. "I took care of that. I rented that small conference room at the inn. The one with the fireplace."

Cinnamon stared at him. "You did what? The whole room?"

He laughed, glad he could surprise her. His pride was taking enough of a beating. "Don't make it sound as if it is a hundred-seat place. I don't think the whole space handles more than thirty. And you did like the fireplace. I told the proprietress we needed some peace. She's serving lunch in there in exactly thirty minutes."

Cinnamon didn't know what to say. Ben's impulses were a constant source of amazement. He didn't know the meaning of restraint. If he wanted to do something he did it. He wasn't afraid of grand gestures—of making himself look less a man. She had never met anyone who was so sure of himself without being arrogant. Nor had she ever met anyone who put her wishes and needs first. He didn't take from her; he gave. And most of the time she didn't know how to return the favor.

"Thank you," she whispered, wishing she could touch him.

"You're welcome, honey," he whispered back, then smiled. "I take it you like my surprise?"

"I wish I could show you how much. You spoil me."

"I'm trying," he admitted. He stuffed and sealed the last envelope and sat back with a sigh. "I'm done."

Cinnamon completed her stack a moment later. "So am I. And to think I promised myself the last time I did this I would never do stuffing again." She rubbed her back, grimacing a little at the stiffness.

Ben rose and extended his hand. "Come on, my tired campaign worker. Talk to me nice and I'll give you one of my extra-special back rubs. Two glasses of wine for lunch, and believe me, you will feel like a new woman." He urged her toward the door, waving to the few people who looked up at their passing.

"What you mean is that I'll be so limp you'll be able to pour me into a thimble." Cinnamon sighed, glad to be escaping, if only for a little while.

Ben glared at one of the staff as he headed toward them, clearly intent on detaining Cinnamon. The man blinked, stopping short. Ben shot a quick look at Cinnamon to see if she noticed. She was busy with her coat and had missed the byplay. This time they were going to get out of the madhouse and have a normal lunch. He didn't care if Metcalf fell off the side of the world. Cinnamon needed a break.

"Come on, let's get out of here before someone misses us." He caught her elbow and all but pushed her out the door.

Cinnamon had no choice but to go. She frowned at him as he half pulled her down the sidewalk toward his car. "Are you that hungry?" she demanded.

"Determined. I want some time alone. Don't you recognize frustration when you see it?" he demanded in turn, stuffing her into the front seat of the car. "I know you. One question and you would have been elbow deep in politics. A man could get jealous that way."

Cinnamon shot him a skeptical look. "You're not serious." His searing glance told her that he was. "But why?"

"Figure it out." He was in no mood to explain the facts of life to her. This once he wanted her to think beyond the physical attraction and find the deeper truth. He needed her complete trust. He was giving her his own, and his protection—although she didn't know that. He wanted the same from her. He needed the security of knowing that she wanted more from him than his prowess in bed.

Cinnamon studied him, wondering at the abrupt mood switch. She had tried telling herself his change-ability was really just her being oversensitive. Now she wasn't so sure. She sighed, rubbing her forehead with the tips of her fingers. Now she was getting a head-ache to go along with her backache.

"Ben, I can't handle cryptic remarks right now. There is too much going on in my life. If you have something to say, then say it."

"What's the point? You aren't ready to hear it, or I wouldn't need to spell it out." Ben turned the car into the inn's parking lot.

The inn was a rustic postcard picture that promised a welcome and peace for the weary traveler. Snow, glistening in the sun, lay on the gabled roof. The sky was blue—more a summer shade than winter gray. Smoke curled from the chimney in a lazy trail. The scene would have been romantic. He had planned it that way. He had wanted to give her pleasure. Yet, he needed some of that romance for himself. Cinnamon. Delicious, sexy, sensual: all that he wanted in a woman. And willfully blind—to him, to herself. She didn't want to know there was more between them than sex. She wouldn't allow herself to need him, to lean on him more than she did already. She wouldn't trust him to help her. Emotion gathered and co-alesced into a feeling too intense to restrain.

"Let's go in." He needed an outlet. Getting out of the car, he strode around to her side, his huge steps eating up the ground. Before Cinnamon, he had been long on patience. But no more. His needs were spurs to his control.

"I don't understand you."

He guided her through to the conference room, pausing only to nod to the owner on duty at the desk. "That's not difficult to tell. You feel safer being in ignorance." He dropped her arm the moment the door closed behind them. Walking to the bay window, he looked out over the snow-covered hills. "When will you stop pretending we're no more than bed partners?"

Not expecting this attack, Cinnamon had no defense prepared. "I don't know what you mean."

Ben swung around. He had to make her understand. Time was running out. He could feel it with every instinct he possessed. "You mean you don't *want* to know what I'm talking about. Tell me about those phone calls. I think you know who's making them and why. I think you're scared half out of your mind. That worries me. You aren't a woman to jump at shadows. So, who is it? What's the threat? And why won't you let me help you? Do you doubt my ability? You trust me with Don's life but not your own. Security is my business. That only leaves one conclusion: you don't want me involved this deeply in your affairs. Do you have any idea how that makes me feel?" His lips twisted at her pained expression. He ignored the hand that she extended and the hoarse "No" that passed her lips. "I'm good enough to sleep with but not to share with."

Cinnamon felt as if she had been slapped. His expression told of more torture than his words. "I didn't think..." she whispered, appalled to realize that it was true. She had been so busy reveling in the feelings he brought to her life, she hadn't considered his side of their relationship.

"Think now." He wouldn't weaken. The tears welling in her eyes would not soften him.

"I'm not used to sharing."

"We've been over this before. Don't fall back on things we both know and understand. Talk to me about *now*. Just what do I have to do to prove myself worthy of your trust?" He stalked over to her, grabbing her arms, his fingers digging through the thickness of her coat to feel the living flesh beneath. "Tell me."

A knock on the door couldn't have been more inconveniently timed. He swore and let her go. Cinnamon turned so that her back was to the entrance. She had to get herself under control. Ben had brought her to tears once more. She hated the weakness but was helpless to fight it. Because he hurt, she was hurting. She was a fool. What good did it do to protect herself if she was going to feel pain anyway? Better to withdraw completely. She glanced over her shoulder when she heard the last of the waiters depart. Ben stood leaning against the door, watching her. The knowledge of what she was thinking was in his eyes. He knew her too well. Feeling vulnerable, she hit back.

"I never said you weren't important to me. I can't help the conclusions you draw. But I don't owe you anything. I give what I can. It's up to you to be satisfied." She started to move toward the table set for two in front of the fire.

He caught her before she could reach it. "You've escaped with that reasoning once too often. Think of something better."

Cinnamon threw back her head, glaring at him. "I don't have to."

Angered, Ben fought the urge to shake her. "Lord, woman, you're stubborn. Tell me about those calls. I want to help. If it makes you feel any better, think of it as my job. Whoever it is could be a threat to your precious senator or his family."

"She is not." It was Cinnamon's turn to swear.

Ben pounced on the pronoun. "'She'? You *do* know her. Is she someone from your past? Does she have some kind of hold over you? Are you afraid of her or what she can do?" His fingers flexed with temper and frustration.

Cinnamon tore out of his grasp and took three quick paces back. Her gaze held his across the small space. Her breath came in short pants. Fear, anger and despair made her voice hoarse. "The only one she wants is me. Don is in no direct danger."

"What the devil do you mean, 'no direct danger'?" He started to close the distance between them.

Caught up in memories of the past, Cinnamon read a different kind of motive in his actions. She felt the shiver of fear a second before she sidestepped him and bolted for the door. Ben reacted out of long years of training. He grabbed her, his arm slipping around her waist to lift her off her feet. Cinnamon fought him, struggling wildly. After the first move, Ben's only aim was to quiet her and protect them both from her well-directed attack. Finally, in desperation, he tossed her on the couch, coming down beside her, his left leg thrown over hers. Stretching her arms high above her head, he glared into her furious eyes.

"Stop this before you hurt one of us, you little fool."

"I hate you."

"Right now I'm not too fond of you, either," he admitted, grunting when her determined efforts to dislodge him connected with a sensitive part of his anatomy. "I said stop it before I have to do something more than just hold you," he commanded harshly.

Cinnamon froze not because of the words but for the truth of his claim. He wasn't hurting her. If there were any bruises to be counted, they were all his. Horrified, she stared at him. The tears that had threatened came back in triplicate. They spilled over, raining down her face.

"I'm sorry. I hate violence. I thought I was protecting myself." Apology, emotions and reasons. The tangle of words expressed the confusion of feelings.

Ben released her hands slowly, his fingers stroking her arms as he lifted her against him. His frustration died at the sight of her expression. "Reflexes are damnable things. They keep us safe, but we lose control over them because they are so ingrained that we forget," he whispered, giving her the only comfort he thought would help. He brushed her hair back from her face. "Corner anyone and they strike back somehow. I should have remembered your courage and your independence. My mistake, too."

"You're more than I deserve."

"I'm no saint." Cinnamon humble was an image he couldn't accept. "I make my own share of mistakes, and most of them seem to be with you." The biggest one of all was the lie she didn't know lay beneath them.

Cinnamon leaned her head back against his shoulder, savoring the peace after the storm. "I need to think, and I'm too tired right now. Give me a day. Old habits are hard to break. And this time I have to get past memories." It was the only promise she could make. Would it be enough?

Ben wanted to demand that she give in now. But he could feel the effort she was making. Her body was stiff. She felt as though she were locked in a battle with herself she thought he couldn't see. "All right." He kissed the crown of her head before laying his cheek against her hair. He had his own decision to make. It was time he told her the truth. If she could take the risk with her past, then he could do no less with his future. Jonathon be damned.

Ben leaned back in his chair and stared out the window. It was late—well after midnight. Would Cinnamon tell him the truth? Could he tell her? He shifted restlessly. Three more days before Metcalf arrived. Jonathon was champing at the bit. Ben frowned. It seemed odd that his boss hadn't been in his office when he had called. Odder still that his secretary had been so evasive about his whereabouts. The phone rang. He glanced at it, for one moment hoping it would be Cinnamon. He was lonely. He would settle for hearing her voice, even if he couldn't hold her in his arms.

"Jonathon," he murmured concealing his surprise. "A bit late wouldn't you say?"

"Tell me about it. This is terrible country. Cold as ice, and snow everywhere," he muttered irritably. "The plane was delayed or I would have called sooner."

Ben sat up with a jerk. "What plane?" A stupid question, but the best he could come up with under the circumstances.

Jonathon ignored the demand. "I want to see you. I've decided to handle this situation myself. None of you have gotten anywhere with this woman. It's time to bring a little pressure to bear. If you can't do it, I will. National security may be at stake here."

"You're out of your overzealous mind. You're so accustomed to looking for flies in the pudding, you can't see the nose on your face. I know her file doesn't check out. But other than that, what evidence do you have? You haven't got one shred despite your ballooned stakeout budget. She hasn't contacted anyone. She hasn't passed any state secrets or *any* secrets, for that matter. All you can get her on is an uncanny ability to make her candidate look like the best thing that's happened to this country since the Constitution."

"I am not interested in your opinion. My actions are sanctioned by a higher authority than yours and I take orders just like you do. So, get over here before I have you relieved of this assignment." Jonathon snapped out the address before hanging up.

Ben slammed down the phone and surged to his feet. He snatched his coat off the bed as he stalked to the door. Time had just run out for Cinnamon and for him.

Eleven

Τhat was quick," Jonathon observed as he opened the door.

"Cut the sarcasm. I'm not in the mood." Ben stalked by to take a chair in the plain little room. He glanced around indifferently. It was no more and no less than he expected from Jonathon.

Jonathon walked over and took the other chair at the round table under the single window. Heat blew gently from the grate at his elbow. He focused on Ben's angry face.

"She got to you, too." He sighed and shook his head. "I hadn't anticipated that. How did she do it?"

Ben sat back, recognizing the tactics. Jonathon would lay on the guilt, then make an appeal to Ben's patriotism or sense of honor. "She didn't try anything. She simply isn't what you believe. I'll grant you she's hiding something. At a guess, I'd say she assumed her old roommate's identity when she died. That's why her background and age seem a little off. That's why she tried to avoid the subject and keep herself out of the real limelight. I'll even grant you she's probably smart enough to pull off a puppet president. The thing is she isn't dishonest enough."

"You think a woman who would hide behind another's identity is above feathering her own nest?" Jonathon stared at him as though he had taken leave of his senses.

Ben's temper rose. He controlled it, even though his hands itched to make forceful contact with Jonathon's jaw. "The one thing we didn't turn up in all our checking was any unexplained income."

"You know as well as I do that she could have hidden any assets if she'd wanted to. It's been done before."

"But you couldn't find it. And in this country, you can't convict someone on suspicion alone."

"But you can bring some pressure. The primary is in a week. Do something."

"No."

For the first time since Ben had known him, Jonathon lost his composure enough to gape. "What do you mean, 'No'?"

Ben smiled. It wasn't a nice gesture. "Never heard the word before?"

"Cut the smart mouth and explain."

"I mean I won't have any more to do with this witch-hunt. You want Cinnamon on a stake, do your own dirty work. As of now, I'm officially out of the picture." He leaned forward to prop his elbows on the table. His smile widened as Jonathon sat back abruptly. "To hurt her you'll have to go through me."

"You're threatening me?"

"What do you think?" Ben got to his feet, knowing that if he stayed much longer he would do more than *think* about knocking some sense into Jonathon.

Cinnamon came out of the shower, a towel wrapped around her body. The phone rang as she reached for the nightshirt she usually wore when traveling, although at home she preferred the freedom of sleeping in nothing but her skin. Her mind was more on Ben and the upcoming election, and she answered absently.

"Don't hang up, Ellen, honey. I want to talk to you."

Cinnamon froze at the voice, more prepared this time to handle her mother, Lydia, than she had been before. "What do you want?"

The soft laugh was low and familiar. Cinnamon shivered at the memory, then forced it away. Her mother had a habit of finding and using any weakness. "To talk to my daughter. To see you. Talk over old times."

"Dream on. The only thing I want from you is silence and absence."

"I had to leave, baby. There were things..." Lydia's voice trailed off, leaving behind a tantalizing tail to be pulled.

Cinnamon waited for more, but nothing was forthcoming. "I can't think of one reason that a real mother would allow her only child to be made an orphan. And we both know what kind of mother you were." Cinnamon sat down on the bed, surprised to find each word was a breath of freedom from the pain, both physical and mental, she had carried for years. "I'm not a child you can bully anymore. You left me to fend for myself after you almost destroyed me. I learned how to survive. There is nothing between us anymore."

"Prove it." The voice was a soft purr; a dare cloaked in velvet.

Cinnamon's reply was equally gentle, her husky tones holding more depth and strength than her mother's ever had. "How? A face-to-face meeting? That's how this goes, isn't it? Then you're going to threaten me somehow. I assume you know about Cinnamon, or you wouldn't have found me."

Lydia inhaled sharply, for once on the receiving end of someone else's power and strength. "Smart, baby. I think I'm proud of you."

Cinnamon ignored the compliment. She was free. Elation filled the places where fear and pain had once dwelt. The frightened child had grown up and into her own. Suddenly a confrontation was important. "Where?"

"The park, about three miles from your hotel. It's closed now. We should be able to talk without interruptions—especially from that oh-so-sexy Ben Forsythe."

The mention of Ben's name caught Cinnamon by surprise, but she was careful not to show it. "When?"

"An hour. And Ellen, come alone or I won't come at all. And you'll find tomorrow morning's papers filled with a lot of nasty little stories you would rather see in the fire."

Cinnamon stared at the phone in her hand, the dial tone indicating that Lydia had hung up. She'd do it, too. Lydia would destroy anyone she could, just for the fun of it. Her child's memory was clear on the strength of Lydia's threat. But Cinnamon had one advantage that Lydia couldn't possibly know. Having

Ben in her life had taught her the meaning of trust—
of trusting herself and others who mattered to her. She
had spent her life, running from shadows of the past.
She had taken another woman's name to escape and
held on to the identity when the need for it was over.
She had shunned the spotlight as much as possible
while pursuing her dream. She'd spent her days looking over her shoulder in case someone should discover her secrets. Now the moment of discovery was
at hand and it didn't matter any longer. When she was
done with Lydia she would go to Ben clean, free, able
to give him the trust he needed and was prepared to
give her.

Cinnamon got to her feet, welcoming the meeting.
She glanced at the phone, wishing she could call Ben
right now and tell him. He would come with her,
standing by her side but not taking her moment from
her. She turned away with regret, knowing that she
had begun alone and had to finish alone. It took only
a moment for her to pull on a pair of jeans, a thick
sweater, fur-lined boots and a down jacket. She
reached the door just as the phone rang. She half
turned, wanting to answer it in case it was Ben, then
changed her mind. He was getting to know her too
well. If it were Ben, then he would sense that something was different. Whether she wanted his company
or not, he would come. Shutting her ears to the insis-
tent ringing, she closed the door and headed for her
car.

Ben swore when the tenth ring went unanswered.
With Jonathon on the loose, he didn't have a moment to waste. He had to be the one to tell Cinnamon
of his real role in her life. He had hoped for more time.
But the sands in the hourglass had run out. Jonathon

was capable of telling Cinnamon in the worst possible way, banking on shock value to loosen her tongue and slip under her guard. No matter what the cost, he had to block the man. Ben slammed down the phone, glaring at it. He would go over to Cinnamon's room and wait. She wouldn't be gone long. She had to meet Metcalf's plane at seven in the morning, attend a news conference at eight and a luncheon with the women's league at noon. The cocktail greeting party at campaign headquarters would round out a jam-packed day. With a schedule like that, Cinnamon would want her rest.

Cinnamon maneuvered the rented car carefully over the lightly snow-covered road. The darkness was almost complete. The beam of the headlights caught the drifting flakes and made the snow shine briefly before they found their death on the warmer metal of the hood. The sign for the park rose out of the black night. The road beside it was not as clear as the one she had been traveling. Cinnamon pulled to a stop at the first picnic table and turned off her lights. She hadn't seen a sign of another car. Minutes ticked by. The snow continued to fall. A shadow moved. Cinnamon strained her eyes. A second later she could pick out the figure moving slowly toward her. Cinnamon pulled her jacket around her as she slipped from the car to face Lydia.

"You've grown up," Lydia observed, coming to a stop before her.

Cinnamon stared at the woman who had given her such bad memories. She remembered her as tall and imposing. The truth was she was little more than five feet four or five. Her voice wasn't nearly as forceful as Cinnamon remembered. Lydia looked every one of her forty-five years and more. Her eyes were a faded version of Cinnamon's own. Her figure beneath the bulky clothes was anyone's guess. Cinnamon expected hate and found nothing—no emotion of any kind. Lydia was a stranger in all ways but name.

"What did you expect?" Cinnamon asked indifferently.

"Someone who looked like me although younger." Lydia shrugged before glancing at the car. "It's cold out here."

Cinnamon nodded but made no move to take the subtle hint to get into the compact. "We don't have much to say, so it doesn't matter."

Lydia glared, and hunched against the wind. "Oh, I think we do. I did my homework, you see. I know all about you, little girl. I know about your lover and his little wife and I know about that hunk, Ben. I know you're sleeping with both men. But do *they* know it?"

Cinnamon laughed, too surprised to do anything else. She had come prepared to face the lie she lived and found instead an illusion that didn't matter. "That's too stupid for words. If this is an example of your best ammunition, then you are in big trouble." She turned slightly to reach for the car's door handle. "Call me again sometime when you can do better."

Lydia snatched at her hand, furious at the brush-off. "Oh, no, you don't. I want my piece of the action. As your mother, I've earned it."

Cinnamon stared at her, unable to believe that even Lydia would have the effrontery to suggest something so outrageous. "You're crazy."

"Crazy? Crazy!" Lydia shrieked, yanking Cinnamon around to face her. She raised her hand, then dropped it quickly when Cinnamon drew herself to her full height, daring her to strike out. "Damn you. I need money and you have plenty. I want my share."

"In your dreams, Lydia. I don't have any money, and even if I did, you don't *deserve* anything but what you have sowed for yourself. I'll do nothing to help or hinder you. You simply don't exist. The best and the worst thing I can think to say to you is that you get back everything you have given to anyone who has ever come in contact with you." Cinnamon pulled her arm from Lydia's suddenly slack fingers. "Do your worst." Without waiting to see how Lydia took her challenge, Cinnamon got into the car and drove away.

Ben. His name and his image were in her mind. She needed him. She wanted him. She had to tell him that the past was finally losing its grip on her mind and her heart. The drive back to the hotel was agonizingly slow. She went first to his room, frowning when she discovered he wasn't there. Where would he go at this time of night, she wondered as she entered the elevator.

"Ms. Cartier?"

Cinnamon blinked, focusing on the distinguished-looking man sharing the compartment with her. "Yes," she murmured, searching her memory for a name to go with the face. There wasn't one.

"I was wondering if I might take a few moments of your time. I think we have some things to discuss."

Cinnamon tensed, not liking the familiar way the man watched her, as if he knew all about her and didn't like what he knew. "I don't know you."

"But I know you." Jonathon reached into his pockets and withdrew a folded paper. He handed it to her, along with his identification.

Cinnamon looked the papers over carefully. Jonathon Strang. The name was familiar. Then she remembered: he was Ben's boss. Some of her tension eased. "Ben works for you," she said, glancing up in time to catch his surprised expression.

"He told you about me?"

Unease started to build. There was something in the man's tone that made her want to run. Cinnamon held her ground, feeling worried but not showing it. Apparently this was a night for confrontation.

"Only that he worked for you."

The elevator stopped, the door opened. Cinnamon stepped out before she realized they had bypassed her floor. Jonathon's hand on her arm prevented her from reentering the elevator. "I really think you should come with me."

"And if I don't?" she asked, bracing herself to make a break for it if necessary.

"Then you will see me tomorrow in a much more official capacity. With the senator and his lovely wife present, as well."

Cinnamon considered taking her chances, but the look in his eyes stopped her. Whatever was wrong, was serious. And Ben was involved.

"All right."

Jonathon released her with a nod. "My hotel isn't far from here."

Cinnamon walked beside him to a nondescript rental car, trying to find an answer to the puzzle. She was no closer to a clue when she entered a small motel that just missed being called cheap. The accommodations were little more than a closet with a bed.

"Just who are you? And don't give me that wide-eyed look of innocence and tell me that fictitious name Cinnamon Cartier. She's dead, according to Ben. We haven't been able to find out your real name yet but we will. So make it easy on yourself and tell me now. I expected Ben to do a better job than this. He's the best with unsolvable puzzles.''

Cinnamon looked at him without seeing him. Instincts she should have heeded supplied pieces of the recent past, rearranging them in new, frightening ways. Ben. Betrayal. Two words. A hurt too deep to heal. Trust. Ben had stood before her and demanded her trust, and all the time he was playing her like a hungry trout on a fishing line for this little creep. He had used her. Seduced her. Taken more from her than she had ever given to a man or anyone. She inhaled sharply, fighting for control of the anger building within her. Where there had been softness, there were now diamond-keen edges.

She had lost more than she had known she had to give. For the first time in her life the future didn't matter. She had no reason to see tomorrow or even to care that the sun rose. "I don't believe in 'easy.' You want me? Find out who I am yourself." Hadn't she learned anything? She hated lies. She'd lived them because she had no choice.

"I don't like theatrics." Jonathon got to his feet, unable to believe she would walk away just like that.

"I don't indulge in them. I leave that to others. To snoopers like you and your little spies." She headed for the door. "You'll know where to find me. I don't run. Not anymore."

Pride, as cold and as deep as the night itself, got her out of the motel room. She caught a taxi back to her room. Still angry, she got into the elevator and to her room. Pain and rage were in her eyes as she faced the man who waited there for her.

"First my mother, then your boss. It only needed you to make this night complete."

Ben got to his feet, watching her warily. She knew the truth. The rage in her was worse than he expected, deeper, colder and infinitely more lethal. He noted the reference to her mother but he ignored it for the moment.

"What did Jonathon tell you?" he asked quietly, without moving closer.

Cinnamon leaned against the door, her arms straight at her sides. The lighting was kind to his lying face. She wondered if he had planned to let his boss break the news, then decided it didn't matter. A lie was a lie.

"Does it make any difference? He told me enough to know that I was just a job to you. I made love with a liar and a betrayer. A Judas." She shrugged, seeing the words sink into his flesh like talons. She had never enjoyed hurting anyone. Her memories had taught her kindness rather than bitterness. Tonight she learned a different lesson. She found that she was capable of revenge.

Ben tensed against the pain, looking beyond the verbal darts to the wound aching below. Jonathon had done his work too well. Whatever trust had begun to build in Cinnamon was gone, killed by the lies he had told and the man who hadn't looked beneath the surface to see the honesty of the woman he suspected of treachery.

"Lying with you in my arms was no lie."

Cinnamon laughed harshly. "It was no truth, either. A man can feel desire without emotion. I'm not a fool, although I've been giving a very good imitation of one lately. I trusted you." The pain ripped through her, tightening her voice and her body.

Ben took a step closer, stopping when her hand came up in an abrupt gesture to ward him off.

"Touch me, and I'll do something we both will regret. I want you out of my room and out of my life." Inner turmoil was tearing at the bars of her restraint. She couldn't take much more. She hurt so badly— worse than she ever had in her life. She needed a target. Denying her need was weakening her control. In a moment she would lose herself and all that she had built from the ashes of the past.

"I had a job to do." Time was slipping through his fingers like sand. Cinnamon was burning every bridge he had tried to make. "I never believed you were capable of manipulating a man into the presidency for someone to control."

The sheer shock of his words caught Cinnamon unprepared. She stared at him, hardly able to believe he would say such a thing. "What?"

"He didn't tell you? I would have thought he would." Ben's lips twisted in a grimace of anger and pain. "That's what prompted my intervention. The powers that be were getting nervous when a little female nobody could turn a hick senator no one had ever heard of into a prime candidate for the presidency. No one would believe that guts and determination could beat the big guys. There had to be a better reason." Ben raked his hand through his hair, wishing he knew some magic words to convince her.

"I'm a troubleshooter of sorts. They called me in. I didn't want the job—refused it until I saw the videotape they had done of you and the Metcalfs at that fund-raiser in Memphis. I won't apologize for what I did. If it hadn't been me, it would have been someone else. I saw your face. I wanted to know the woman with such power, such courage. I didn't believe or disbelieve the motives behind the investigation. Then I met you, got to know you. I made my decision then.

I never tried to prove you guilty. At first I tried to find the facts, and later I wanted you to be innocent. But it wouldn't have mattered. For the first time in my life, it wouldn't have mattered. I would have taken you even if you had done all they suspected." He closed the distance between them to grab her arms.

"Do you have any idea what knowing that did to me? The one thing that has kept me sane in my business is my belief in honesty and principle. For you, I would have given up both." He released her abruptly, turning away. He had lost. There was no understanding, no softness in her now. Her eyes were empty. Her body was rigid.

Cinnamon stared at his back, reeling from the angry words that had spilled out. Nothing made sense. Nothing. She didn't know what to believe. She didn't know whom to trust, what to feel, what to say. She hurt. Ben had lied. The "truth" wasn't the truth at all. The world she had begun to see was an illusion. Wrapping her arms around her middle, she tried to make sense of something, anything. No words came.

Ben walked to the chair and collected his coat. "I can't take back the lies, but I can see that Jonathon doesn't win." He turned to look at her. The expression on her face would haunt him forever. There were tears on her cheeks, but he doubted she felt them or even knew that she was crying. "I quit tonight. I came here to tell you who I was and to offer you my help. The offer no longer stands. I'll clear you with or without your help. Like you, I always pay my debts." He shrugged into the coat, his eyes never leaving hers.

"I would have gone with you to see your mother if you had asked me. But I guess that was too much trust for you to manage." He walked toward her, stopping a foot away. "I can't go if you don't move."

Cinnamon searched his eyes, seeing there a pain as deep as her own. "I wanted you there. I almost called."

Ben watched her, holding her words as treasures. Feeling the way she did, she could still give him a gift. Jonathon and his superiors had no idea of the wrong they had done this night.

"I realized I couldn't do it. I had to be free of the past. I had to have the courage to face it and not run. You taught me that." Cinnamon pushed away from the door, feeling intolerably weary.

Ben clenched his hands in an effort to deny the need to reach out to her, to give her his warmth and strength, to hold her while she told him of the meeting. He had forfeited that right, he reminded himself. The price had been the lie.

"Thank you, Cinnamon," he murmured, touching her cheek with one finger. Her flinch went through him like a knife. "That was more than I deserve." He opened the door and stepped into the hall. The urge to look back was overwhelming but he curbed it. Cinnamon wanted nothing from him but his absence.

"My name is Ellen Smith," Cinnamon whispered just before the door closed, separating them.

Twelve

——

Cinnamon stared at her reflection in the mirror, grimacing at the ravages of a sleepless night and the emotional roller coaster she'd been riding. Ben. She hadn't been able to sleep, thinking of how he had held her, loved her, understood her when she hadn't understood herself. At four in the morning, in a cold bed, she had stared at the black night sky and known she loved him. The taste of his betrayal had been like a poison because of that love. If she had cared less, she could have listened to his reasons and perhaps accepted if not understood. But she couldn't forgive him for touching her so deeply and still conspiring with others to spy on her.

Turning away from her reflection, she pulled on her dress and finished preparing herself for the full day ahead. There would be no time to think, to wonder "what if?" She had the twins, and Linda and Don

counting on her. She couldn't let them down. Don had
given her the chance to make her dreams for the future a reality. Linda and the twins had taught her how
loving a family could be. Her own life was a mess, but
theirs was still on track. She needed that knowledge
now more than ever. Don would have his nomination
if it was within her power to help him get it.

Cinnamon arrived at the airport on time, pleased to
see that the reporters gathered were a well-mannered
lot. She smiled, answering questions with outward
ease, while keeping an eye open for Ben or his boss.
She wasn't sure what to believe about Ben's job. And
she certainly wasn't certain what Jonathon was capable of. The plane landed on time. The small press
conference put together in the VIP lounge went off
without a hitch. Cinnamon drove the Metcalfs to the
hotel, listening with half an ear to their news of the
farm that was home base.

"Boys, why don't you go down to the coffee shop
and check out the area," Don suggested as soon as
they entered the suite Cinnamon had reserved for
them.

Cinnamon raised a brow at that maneuver. She
glanced at Linda, surprising a strange look in the older
woman's eyes. "What's wrong?" she asked as soon as
they were alone.

Don took a seat on the couch and gestured for
Linda to join him. "We have something to tell you."

Cinnamon braced herself, not liking the gravity of
his tone. She sat down in the chair facing them, waiting with outer calm while sorting through an endless
list of possibilities.

"I . . . That is, Linda and I have decided to take my
hat out of the ring," Don announced carefully. He
waited for Cinnamon's reaction—which didn't come.

He grimaced slightly as she continued to look at him. "Linda and I wanted this chance, as you know. If it hadn't been for you we wouldn't have had it. But the truth is I realize I'm not made for the presidency. I'm not tough enough or sharp enough. Linda and the boys will always come first with me. That's all right for a senator but not for the commander in chief."

The world had stopped. Cinnamon knew it. Her future was shot down without a whimper. The irony of Don's timing couldn't have been better. She smiled slightly, feeling light-headed and not even sure why. Shock, probably. She'd certainly had more than her share.

Don stared at her before exchanging looks with his wife.

"We know this has to be a surprise to you," Linda began worriedly, leaning forward to take Cinnamon's hand.

Cinnamon laughed softly. "This must be my week for them," she agreed. With the best will in the world, she couldn't control her amusement. Better to laugh than to cry, she assured herself. "When do you want to make the announcement?"

"Tonight. The primary is only a week away."

"Are you throwing your support anyone's way, or are you leaving it up for grabs?" The practicalities had to be dealt with before she could escape.

Don named his chief rival. "What do you think?"

"A good man. Sharp and fairly honest." She nodded as she pulled her notebook from her briefcase and began jotting down a list of things to do. If she kept her mind busy enough, she could push the destruction of her plans and concern about her future away until she was strong enough to deal with them.

"Do you want to use the reasons you gave me, or gild the lily?"

Don shrugged and looked vaguely uncomfortable. "I thought you would be angry or at least surprised," he murmured, ignoring her question.

"Three days ago I might have been," she admitted without lifting her head. "But I don't think anything could surprise me for at least a year from now." She made another note, then continued. "I think we'd better stick with the truth. Much more effective, and it certainly fits your image."

"Cinnamon, what will you do?" Linda asked.

"Do?" Her head lifted at that. "Keep on doing what I've been doing. Why? Are you planning on firing me?" The last she directed at Don.

"Of course not." He scowled irritably. "But there is no sense in fooling myself. You're meant to make more of a splash in this game than I ever will. I feel like I've let you down. I want to help get you hooked up with someone who can give you the scope I can't."

Cinnamon felt emotion stir under the layers of her weariness. She fought for control. To open the door to even the smallest feeling meant drowning in the deluge of pain. "I think maybe I'll take a short vacation. I haven't had one in a while. Then I'll decide."

"In an election year?" Don stared at her in shock.

Linda touched his arm. "It's her life, honey. Cinnamon knows what's best for her." She smiled at Cinnamon. "You know we want to see you on top, but only if you want it, too."

Cinnamon got to her feet. "I've got a lot to do, so I'll be on my way." She reached the door and turned. "This is going to be a nine-day wonder. It will start when I cancel the luncheon for this morning. I would suggest not answering the phone. I'll tell the desk to hold your calls, as well."

Don came to her and took her hand. "You do what is best. We'll follow your lead."

Ben stared at the notes in front of him that had taken him all morning and quite a number of phone calls to get. Cinnamon's—no, make that Ellen Smith's—life lay before him. Even Jonathon would have to admit that the facts fit. The worst anyone could say of Cinnamon/Ellen was that she had worked for unreported wages for four years of her life. Not that it really mattered. She had made so little money she would have gotten all her withholding back, had she filed. Poor kid.

More than ever he admired the woman Cinnamon had become. He couldn't call her Ellen. The name just didn't fit. He wondered if it ever had. There was fire and ambition in Cinnamon. She was a woman who made her life, not just lived it. He understood her better now, understood the depth of her sense of betrayal now that he could see her history—the times she had reached out and been denied. It was a wonder she had come to him at all, had trusted him enough to talk, to give herself in passion.

Folding the paper very carefully, he rose and pulled on his coat. He had a problem to solve for his woman. Jonathon was a threat, only because he was such a rule follower and as stubborn as a mule when he got an idea in his head. But the man wasn't vindictive. Faced with the facts, he would back off. First he would see Jonathon and then, if necessary, Metcalf. Finally he would tackle Cinnamon.

Nothing was ever as easy as it sounded. For once in his life, the adage was proving false. Ben watched

Jonathon as he read the information on Ellen Smith, alias Cinnamon Cartier.

"Damn."

Ben blinked at the oath coming from Jonathon. The man never swore—never raised his voice, for that matter.

"Of all the stupid, ill-advised wild-goose chases, this one takes the cake. We do anything about this and all of us are going to look the fool. We had to dig deep just to find out who she is. Now she looks like a flaming nun done in by the Washington bureaucrats. How did she do it? College at night and day. How did she eat, much less manage to graduate in the top three of her class? And with a mother like that and God only knows who her father was. Runaway at sixteen. It's a wonder she didn't fall into some pimp's hands at that age—or worse."

Jonathon dropped the paper on the table and got to his feet to pace the room. "No wonder she all but told me to take a flying leap," he grumbled irritably. "I don't like being made a fool of. Somebody's head is going to roll for this, and it won't be mine."

Ben got to his feet, not really caring who got whom in the mess. "What about Cinnamon? Is she in the clear now?"

"Don't be a fool. Of course." Jonathon swung around, glaring. "I wish I had never heard of that crazy woman."

Ben controlled his temper with effort. "I think she deserves something out of this. Something more than permission to go on with her life."

Jonathon's eyes narrowed. "Meaning?"

"I want you to fix her past. I want you to make her name or any other she might want to choose as legal as the law demands, and I want it in writing or the next best thing that there will be no repercussions to her alias.''

''Or?''

''I don't think you want to go into that.'' Ben crossed his arms, watching his boss struggle with his regulation conscience.

''It will take time.''

Ben shook his head. ''No, it won't. You've got the clout. Use it.''

Jonathon shifted, glared then shrugged. ''All right. But I don't like it.''

''You and your bosses would have liked a personal, public apology to the lady less. She made us all look like idiots. Not a nice image.''

Ben started for the door.

''What will you do?''

He glanced over his shoulder. ''I'm off the payroll now. I don't have to answer that.''

''You're going after her,'' Jonathon persisted.

''Yes.'' Ben slammed the door on his answer. He was going after her but he didn't have a lot of hope in getting her anytime soon. How he was going to win back her trust was beyond him. He might be able to give the life she had led reality, but he couldn't take away her memories.

He got into the car and turned on the radio. He needed something to keep his mind off his thoughts while he waited for the time out of Cinnamon's busy schedule to confront her, to try to make her see reason.

''We interrupt this program for a special news bulletin. Senator Donald Metcalf, one of the forerunners in the bid for the Democratic nomination for the presidency has just announced his withdrawal from the New Hampshire primary, Senator Metcalf is throwing . . .''

Ben tuned the rest of the announcement out as he touched the accelerator and headed for Metcalf's hotel. He foolishly hadn't thought to ask Jonathon if he had spoken to Metcalf. He would enjoy taking Jonathon apart for this, he promised himself as he pulled into the parking lot. The sight of three news vans in the area increased his anger. His strides ate up the asphalt as he crossed the expanse and entered the lobby. Reporters were milling around. He overheard snatches of their conversation.

''Where's Cartier . . .? He's never without her . . . No one's seen her since the senator made the announcement . . . Heard she quit.''

A chill ran down Ben's spine at the speculation. Cinnamon wasn't a woman to quit. What had Jonathon and he done between them? The elevator took him up to the tenth floor with agonizing slowness. The sight of two security men on duty outside the Metcalf suite wasn't reassuring. Neither was the way they scrutinized his identification before allowing him to enter.

''Where is she?'' he demanded as soon as he was alone with Metcalf.

''I don't know. She stayed with us until the press conference was over. Then she handed me a list of the things she had done and told me she was leaving. I tried to stop her.'' Don shrugged, looking uncomfortable, harassed and not a little weary. ''I had no idea she would take my decision so hard.''

Ben's eyes narrowed. ''Your decision.'' With the best will, he couldn't keep the edge out of his voice. Donald didn't notice.

"I can't take the pace. My family is too important to me. I found out I didn't want my dreams at their expense."

"Was that the only reason?"

Donald stared at him. "Of course. I don't lie," he said simply.

Ben turned and walked out of the room. Where would she go to ground? Her whole life was crumbling around her ears. Where would she go to be safe?

Cinnamon stared out the plane window, deliberately thinking of nothing but the immediate arrangements for getting home. She was lucky she had been able to get a flight out so quickly. The reporters hadn't found her as yet. With luck she would be packed and gotten out of the apartment before anyone realized she had flown the coop. She couldn't face the questions that were sure to be waiting for her. The public always had to know all the gory details, and Ben's betrayal had stolen her defenses. Her mother was breathing down her neck. There was nowhere to hide. So she was running and she wasn't even sure where. For the second time in her life she was leaving without a goal or a destination.

The plane began its descent. Cinnamon looked out over the capital and said her goodbyes. She wouldn't be coming back. That much she did know.

Her apartment was cold and empty. She didn't care, nor did she turn on the heat. She wouldn't be there long enough for the temperature to make any difference. She had lived most of her life out of a suitcase. The furniture was rented. There were no mementos—nothing beyond the rest of her clothes and a few linens to pack. And she was a world-class packer. The cases were filled and lined up at the door in less than an hour. The calls to the rental company and the utilities were completed. The key had been returned to the manager on the first floor. The food from the refrigerator was donated to her next-door neighbor. She was finished with Washington and all it stood for.

She took one more tour of the apartment, stopping at the bedroom to remember because she couldn't forget. She and Ben hadn't made love here, but it didn't seem to matter. She had slept here, dreaming of him and being held in his arms. She had ached with loneliness, her body on fire for wanting him, her mind filled with images she couldn't ignore—images of how tender he had been, of how loved she had felt.

"A lie." She whispered the words in the silence as she leaned her head against the jamb and let the tears fall. She needed to cry. For the moment she was safe here, alone with no one to see or hear her pain, her defeat. She had been a fool. That, in some ways, was harder to stomach than all the rest.

Ben was out of breath by the time he reached Cinnamon's door. An urgent need to find Cinnmon drove him to take the stairs rather than wait for the elevator. If he didn't find her here, he didn't have a clue where to look. Cinnamon had the world to hide in and the courage to start from scratch under another name, making a new niche for herself that had no ties with the past. If he lost her, he could spend a lifetime looking and never find her again.

He closed his hand on the knob, turning it, surprised when it gave way. He stepped into the apartment and almost fell over the six cases lined up beside the door. Sweat popped out on his brow at the sight. So close to losing her! He could feel her presence although the rooms were silent. He moved down the hall, seeing her before he had gone halfway. Her back was to him as she leaned against the jamb, her head bowed. The posture hurt him more than he would have thought possible. She looked so defeated, so lost.

"It's over," he said softly, stopping behind her but not touching her.

Cinnamon stiffened at the sound of his voice. A dream? A nightmare?

"You're in the clear. Jonathon and his little spies are gone. And if you want it, Cinnamon Cartier is your name for real. Or Ellen Smith. Or any other name." He lifted his hand and lightly stroked her hair. He wanted to do more, but he was afraid to reach out. When she didn't flinch or draw away, he allowed his fingers to thread through the shining mass.

"I don't want you here and I don't want your gifts." Cinnamon straightened her shoulders and tried not to feel the warmth of his touch. She didn't want to remember what it felt like to lean on him, to let him into her mind, her heart and her body. She had lost too much already.

"It's not a gift. You earned the right to the name, and your friend gave it to you before I ever could." Ben dropped his hand to her shoulder and turned her toward him. The tears in her eyes sparkled in the sunlight pouring through the windows. But nothing could erase the emptiness of her expression. "Yell at me. I deserve it. Rage. Throw things if you must, but don't stand there beaten. You aren't beaten. I don't think anything on the face of this earth could make you give up."

Cinnamon stared at him, smiling with grim humor. "I don't have to be beaten. I beat myself. I trusted the wrong person. I made a life for myself by learning that people, no matter what their intentions, were rarely around when they were needed. So I learned not to need—until you. I believed you even though I didn't want to. Every instinct I had said not to, but I didn't listen. I wanted you so badly, I believed.''

Her honesty hurt more than anything else could have. Her soul and her heart were laid bare. She made no attempt to evade his touch, nor did she seem to realize he held her.

"And I betrayed you. You can't forgive that.'' He wanted to hold her, for he could feel her slipping away. He wanted to shout out his rage at fate. Without realizing it, he had looked for a lifetime for a woman like Cinnamon. By his own hand he had lost her.

"I can forgive that. It's your job. I know about doing things you have to do when there is no other way.''

Ben understood then, more than he wanted to. The battle he thought he was fighting wasn't the real one.

"It's myself I can't forgive or trust.'' She stared at him, reading the pain that was hers in his eyes. "All my life I looked for something, anything to believe in. Don was honest. He would have been a good president. Maybe a great one. I believed that or I wouldn't have worked for him. I didn't see what was happening to his life. Maybe I didn't want to see because his dream and mine were so tied together.''

How could he help her? Ben had never felt so useless in his life. Every problem, every situation, had a solution. An end. A new beginning.

"You know what's really funny?'' Cinnamon said. "I love you. I knew it last night. But how can I trust the feeling? How do I know it's the truth?'' She searched his eyes, looking for answers.

Ben's fingers tightened on her arms. A spark of hope. She had just handed him a diamond and she didn't seem to know it. "How do any of us know? You want guarantees. I can't give you that. No one can. I love you more than my own honor, but I can't hand you trust on a platter. I can't make you believe in me, yourself or us. And even if I could, you wouldn't let me make it easy for you. You aren't a woman for 'easy.' You live and breathe for challenge, for beating the odds, for winning. You're a gambler trying to live an ordinary life."

Cinnamon let the words pour into her, feeling the emotions begin to seethe below the surface. Love, anger, betrayal, wanting, forgiveness and understanding—but more than all, a tiny bud of hope born out of the fire and ashes of the past.

"How can you be sure?" Her hands came up to encircle his wrists. She didn't notice the gesture, but Ben did.

"I see myself in you. I watch you do what you have to do to survive, and I see a woman who moves through life helping when she had very real reasons to lash out. I see a woman who touched people and tried to give them their dreams when she didn't really believe in dreams herself. I see a woman willing to give herself to a man that she didn't know when her instincts were warning her off. And yet she believed, she trusted and she tried. You ask how to forgive yourself. My question is: why should you want to?"

Cinnamon's vision blurred. "You make me sound special. You don't know what my real life was like."

"You are special and I do know. But more than that, it doesn't matter except that it made you the woman I love. For that, and that alone, I can live with it." His hands framed her face.

"What do you want?"

"All that you are?" No quarter given.

"And I'll get?" Cinnamon faced him and the future, knowing she wanted to believe in him and herself.

"All that I am." He smiled a little, feeling her faint softening. He was winning.

"I don't have a job."

"I don't give a damn what you have or don't have. If all you owned was what you're wearing, I'd take you." He slipped his arms around her, pulling her tightly against his body. "I don't need to work for quite a while. Like you, I've always taken the world on my own terms."

"That doesn't make it better," she whispered, beginning to trust.

"The devil it doesn't. We've earned a long vacation. Spend it with me—a week, a year, a lifetime." He thrust his hips against her, letting her feel the passion growing within him. Her gasp was a delight. He laughed softly, bending to brush her lips with a kiss designed to tease and entice.

"You're talking about forever," Cinnamon murmured, trying to hold on to her sanity when all she wanted to do was forget everything but him.

"I'm talking marriage," he corrected, nipping at her earlobe. "And children. And growing old together. And arguing. And making up. And loving. And being there in the night when the memories get so bad that you want to hold me. Of waking up with my own memories and being able to talk to one who won't turn away because the world isn't the pretty candy store she thinks it is. Of being able to take a risk for the sheer joy of it and knowing you'll see and understand what I'm doing. Of having a partner who isn't afraid to push me to my limits and more." His mouth found hers, taking what she hadn't decided to give. His tongue probed hungrily, demanding her response.

Cinnamon moaned, knowing she couldn't deny either of them any longer. She needed him, and somehow he needed her. He saw in her things that no one else did. He liked the parts of her that might have frightened or intimidated another man. He was her match: a man she could trust.

"Say yes, damn you, or I'll kidnap you until you're too old and gray to run away from me," he promised, raising his head.

Cinnamon's eyes glowed with passion and returning life. "I'll say yes, you arrogant bully. But you may wish I hadn't if you curse at me again."

He grinned, loving the fire in her eyes and the temper that erupted. "That's my woman." He lifted her high in his arms and swung her around before sauntering into the bedroom and tossing her onto the bare mattress. "Let's make love and then let's get out of here before those fool reporters find us. In an hour we can be on a plane to almost anywhere." He came down beside her, his hand cupping her cheek. "Pick a destination."

"Rio."

His brows rose, then he threw back his head and laughed. "Good choice. It's warm down there and they have the most scandalous swimming suits you've ever seen. I'll buy you one, but you can't wear it anywhere but with me."

"They'd better have a male counterpart," she returned, unbuttoning his coat. She pulled his shirt free and pushed the coat and shirt off his shoulders together.

"I just noticed something. It's as cold as a refrigerator in here."

"You'll be warm in a minute. I promise." Cinnamon's eyes gleamed with wicked interest, an expression matched by her chosen mate.

"I will, will I? Sounds interesting. Got some tricks up your sleeve."

"Not my sleeve, lover."

*   *   *   *   *

Coming in July from

Silhouette Desire®

ODD MAN OUT #505
by Lass Small

Roberta Lambert is too busy with her job to notice that her new apartment-mate is a strong, desirable man. But Graham Rawlins has ways of getting her undivided attention....

Roberta is one of five fascinating Lambert sisters. She is as enticing as each one of her three sisters, whose stories you have already enjoyed or will want to read:

- Hillary in GOLDILOCKS AND THE BEHR (Desire #437)

- Tate in HIDE AND SEEK (Desire #453)

- Georgina in RED ROVER (Desire #491)

Watch for Book IV of Lass Small's terrific miniseries and read Fredricka's story in TAGGED (Desire #528) coming in October.

If you missed any of the Lambert sisters' stories by Lass Small, send $2.50 plus 75 cents postage and handling to:

In the U.S.
901 Fuhrmann Blvd.
P.O. Box 1396
Buffalo, NY 14269-1396

In Canada
P.O. Box 609
Fort Erie, Ontario
L2A 5X3

SD505-1

Silhouette Special Edition

presents

★ LOVE AND GLORY ★

from
Lindsay McKenna

Introducing a gripping new series celebrating our men—and women—in uniform. Meet the Trayherns, a military family as proud and colorful as the American flag, a family fighting the shadow of dishonor, a family determined to triumph—with **LOVE AND GLORY!**

June: A QUESTION OF HONOR (SE #529) leads the fast-paced excitement. When Coast Guard officer Noah Trayhern offers Kit Anderson a safe house, he unwittingly endangers his own guarded emotions.

July: NO SURRENDER (SE #535) Navy pilot Alyssa Trayhern's assignment with arrogant jet jockey Clay Cantrell threatens her career—and her heart—with a crash landing!

August: RETURN OF A HERO (SE #541) Strike up the band to welcome home a man whose top-secret reappearance will make headline news . . . with a delicate, daring woman by his side.

If you missed any of the LOVE AND GLORY titles send your name, address and zip or postal code, along with a check or money order for $2.95 for each book ordered, plus 75¢ postage and handling, payable to Silhouette Reader Service to:

In Canada	In USA
P.O. Box 609	901 Furhmann Blvd.
Fort Erie, Ontario	P.O. Box 1396
L2A 5X3	Buffalo, NY 14269-1396

Please specify book title with your order.

LG-1A

Silhouette Desire®

COMING NEXT MONTH

#505 ODD MAN OUT—Lass Small
July's *Man of the Month*, Graham Rawlins, was undeniably attractive, but Roberta Lambert seemed uninterested. However, Graham was very determined, and she found he'd do almost *anything* to get her attention....

#506 THE PIRATE O'KEEFE—Helen R. Myers
Doctor Laura Connell was intrigued by the injured man washed up on her beach. When she discovered his true identity it was too late—she'd fallen for the pirate O'Keefe.

#507 A WILDER NAME—Laura Leone
Luke Swain was positively the most irritating man Nina Gnagnarelli had ever met. He'd insulted her wardrobe, her integrity and her manners. He'd also set her heart on fire!

#508 BLIND JUSTICE—Cathryn Clare
As far as Lily Martineau was concerned, successful corporate lawyer Matt Malone was already married—to his job. Matt pleaded guilty as charged, then demanded a retrial.

#509 ETERNALLY EVE—Ashley Summers
Nate Wright had left Eve Sheridan with a broken heart. Now he seemed to have no memory of her—but it was a night Eve would never forget!

#510 MAGIC TOUCH—Noelle Berry McCue
One magic night with a handsome stranger made Caroline Barclay feel irresistible. But she didn't believe in fairy tales until James Mitchel walked back into her life—as her new boss.

AVAILABLE NOW: